The Oxley Crossing Romances

Book 7

Healing Dr Murphy

LENA WEST

Gymea Publishing

Published by Gymea Publishing

https://www.facebook.com/LenaWestAuthor/

www.lenawestauthor.com

ISBN-13: 978-0-6485978-2-7

Disclaimer

This story is a work of fiction.

Names, characters, places and incidents are the product of the author's imagination and are used fictitiously. Any resemblance to events, locales or actual persons, living or dead, is entirely coincidental.

Some actual locations and events may be referenced in passing.

Table of Contents

Disclaimer iii

Table of Contents iv

Dedication vii

1 1

2 13

3 19

4 27

5 41

6 61

7 77

8 89

9 101

10 117

11 129

12 139

13 145

14 155

15 161

16 169

17 181

18   193

Epilogue   205

Here is Your Preview of *Buried Truth* 208

Other Books by Lena West 219

About the Author 226

HEALING DR MURPHY

Dedication

This book is for Dr Marie, a constant source of encouragement to whom I have turned for answers to medical questions in my books on several occasions. Thank you, Dr Marie, and I hope you enjoy this story.

Lena West

1

Clamping down hard on nerves threatening to escape her control, Kat Murphy cast a deliberately impassive glance round the reception area, ending her survey when a blonde, middle-aged woman entered through a door in the back of the room.

"The old place has changed a lot," Kat commented in a vain attempt to distract herself from the churning in her gut at what awaited her. The tasteful Christmas decorations adorning the lobby were certainly a step up from the dusty, fly-speckled farm calendars which Fred Hayes had considered the height of elegance.

"You and your husband," an assumption based on the sign outside stating P & M Morris to be the licensees, and the woman's nametag reading Marge Morris, "have really put some work in."

"Oh, It was a real work of love. Owning a hotel like this was our dream, and when we saw *The Victoria Inn* we couldn't resist."

Marge bridled, her broad smile proclaiming her pride.

"Especially when Oxley Crossing is such a wonderful town. So much history. Have you been here before, then?"

"Umm. A lifetime ago. Before your time. *The Victoria* was a dump back then."

A lifetime ago, and wasn't that the truth. Scrubbing pots in the kitchen at thirteen. Waiting tables at fifteen. Behind the bar at eighteen, as soon as she was legal. If there was one place in Oxley Crossing Kat knew well, it was *The Victoria Inn*. Almost as well as that drunken bastard Colin Murphy knew it. At least as it had been under Fred Hayes's management. Looked like it might be different now. She couldn't help wondering if the old man had changed too. If he had … and if it was a change for the better …?

But no. Just, no. Not going there. I'll find out soon enough.

Kat redirected her thoughts to the business in hand, refusing to speculate. Knowing daydreams were worthless. Daydreams only led to disappointment when they relied on other people for success. Every single time. It had been a long time since Kat Murphy had relied on anyone else outside of work.

Besides, she'd *never* known Colin Murphy to be a reliable bet when it counted.

"I'd like to book a room please. Not sure how long, but possibly a few nights."

Very few, hopefully. Depending how long it takes me to fulfil my Godforsaken mission and shake the dust of The Crossing off my boots. Again. Forever.

Suddenly all business, Marge brought out the guest register.

"If you'll just sign here, I'll take you up to your room. When you've settled in, feel free to take a look around. We've turned the dining room into a museum space with old photos and such. You might find it interesting since you're familiar with The Crossing as it used to be." Marge Morris turned the guest register of *The Victoria Inn*, Oxley Crossing's historic iron-lace clad hotel, towards her guest.

Familiar with The Crossing! Kat grimaced. *Another understatement.*

Kat picked up the pen and signed under the latest date, Monday, November 4th, 2019 where hers was the only entry. Visitors to The Crossing must still be a rarity. Although, flicking back, she noted the Friday and Saturday had been busier, so maybe not.

"My dear!" Marge, idly reading the name in the register, K M Murphy, gasped. "I'm so sorry. Rattling on here when you must be in a hurry to get to St Catherine's for the funeral."

Now she knew this thirtyish woman, with her short, blond hair and bright hazel eyes was family, Marge could easily discern a familial likeness to Colin Murphy. All the Murphys shared his dimpled chin and those green-brown eyes.

"Funeral? No. I don't know anything about a funeral." Icy fingers tiptoed up Kat's spine. "Who died?"

Please God, not Bridget. Or Pat or Sean.

"You mean you don't know? But I thought … Your name. Murphy. But I guess it's a fairly common surname."

Marge faltered to a halt, debating whether to go on.

Only, there was the name. And the looks. Marge frowned, then nodded decisively.

"Colin and Therese Murphy from here in The Crossing were killed Friday night," she informed her guest, "when their car ran off the road and hit a tree."

Unsure what the churning in her gut portended, Kat took a moment to assimilate the information.

"Colin Murphy? Father of Bridget, Patrick and Sean?" she asked, her already fragile emotions spiralling towards out of control behind the mask of her best poker-face. She bit down on her lip, the sharp pain countering the nausea produced by the answer.

"Yes," Marge nodded, looking distressed. "And the little ones. Were they family after all, dear?"

Kat just nodded, then, regaining her power of speech, muttered, "My father."

"Oh, dear. I feel dreadful being the one to tell you this."

Her head spinning, Kat suppressed the urge to curse. Typical of the Old Bastard. She'd finally decided to mend fences and he upped and died on her. He'd never made things easy for her. Never.

Not knowing who in Hell Therese and the 'little ones' were, she ignored Marge's references to them.

"I've just returned from The States. I've been travelling. Out of touch, so no-one was able to reach me." Although she doubted anyone would have tried very hard. Since she hadn't ever reached out, no-one would have a clue where in the world she'd ended up.

"You say the funeral's today?"

Marge, who'd already noted the twang overlaying her guest's Australian accent, nodded again.

No getting out of it.

Kat was here. She'd have to put in an appearance. Although their father's funeral was the last place she would have chosen to make her peace with Bridget and the boys.

"What time?"

"This is dreadful! Dreadful!" Wringing her hands, Marge pulled herself together. She wished Phil was here, but he'd just headed round to the church himself. She was alone on duty this morning as she hated funerals and never attended one if she could avoid it.

"This is a terrible homecoming for you, dear. I'm so sorry. You'll have to hurry. The funeral's at ten."

The grandfather clock down the hall obligingly chimed the quarter to. A fatalistic glance at her well-worn Texan cowboy boots, black jeans and white silk shirt assured Kat, that while she wasn't really dressed appropriately for a funeral, she'd pass muster in a crowd.

"St Catherine's, you said?"

Marge nodded her head, her directions unheard as Kat strode out, keys in hand, to get back behind the wheel. Eighteen years living in The Crossing, fronting up for Mass at St Catherine's Catholic Church every Sunday morning meant she'd have no trouble finding her way.

~~~~~
~~~~~

"We are gathered here today ..."

The priest, a stranger, not old Father Ahearn of the Hellfire and Brimstone sermons Kat had loathed, began as she entered the church. Automatically dipping her fingers in the Holy Water, she made the sign of the Cross. Genuflecting, she was about to slip into an empty space in the back pew, when she rebelled.

Damn it all! I'm his daughter! I've got the right to sit up front, not cringing away in the back as if I've got something to be ashamed of. I'm done with that.

Moving across to the side aisle, she made her way silently forward, wondering who all the people on the front pews were. There were certainly more than she could account for when she performed a mental roll-call. Slipping in beside a tall, dark-suited man, she sat at the very end of the pew.

Her neighbour turned to see who the late-comer was, his jaw dropping as he recognised her. Now she could see his face, Kat recognised him, too. Her heart stuttered. Maybe the front pew was a mistake. She wasn't ready.

"Bloody Hell, Kat. Where'd you spring from?" he whispered.

"Later Sean." She nudged his elbow, deliberately turning to face the priest who frowned at their interruption, slight though it was.

The muted light shining through dusty stained-glass windows combined with the lingering odour of incense cast Kat back through the years. Assaulted by memories, only ingrained habit ensured she sat, stood and knelt in all the right places. As the service neared its end, she became aware of the sibilant whisperings behind her.

She wished now she had hidden in the back as she had so often in the past.

Her only reason for attending regularly back then was fear of her father's belt around her legs. She'd learnt early to pick her fights. *Did Dad think God only saw him when he knelt piously in front of the altar?* She wondered again, as she often had in the distant past. Although even Colin Murphy couldn't make her take Communion or make her confession to Fr Ahearn. She suspected the 'Black Crow' as she nicknamed him had heard, and believed, the rumours about her and wanted all the salacious details. She'd refused to give him the satisfaction.

Finally, the service was over. Thankfully the short version with only a single, blandly impersonal eulogy, instead of the full Requiem Mass Kat didn't think she could have sat through. The family led the exodus, following the two sealed coffins out the door. Drawing in a deep lungful of the mild fresh air, Kat braced herself for the inevitable.

While most of the congregation headed straight for their cars to drive the short distance to the cemetery on the outskirts of town, a few of the older women who'd recognised the stranger on the family pew as the long-lost Kathleen Murphy, tried to nose their way in to hear her story.

They didn't stand a chance. If there was one thing Murphys were born knowing, it was how to close ranks against outsiders. One icy glare from Bridget, now the senior member of the clan, and the gossipmongers backed off to a respectful distance.

With children, teenagers, and a couple of adults Kat took to be in-laws forming a shield-wall around them, Bridget, Patrick and Sean confronted their sister Kathleen.

"Picked your time for the grand homecoming, didn't you, Kat? If you're hoping for rich pickings, hope on. Dad died as he lived, with empty pockets. There's no money for this shindig, let alone anything else, so be prepared to kick in your share since you've condescended to grace us with your presence."

"Yeah, Sis." Patrick took over from Bridget. "With you here we can split the costs four ways instead of three. Where'd you disappear to, anyway? Where have you been for the last eighteen years?"

Silence reigned as they waited for her response. The Kathleen they remembered would have jumped in, boots and all, defending herself against her siblings' impugned slur.

This Kat simply stood her ground, unable to fault her older siblings' opening salvo. They probably had no more idea what to say than she did, and in the Murphy family money had always been a vitally important subject. A reliable conversational fallback.

Probably because it had been largely non-existent. Still, it looked as if Kat could forget the fatted calf. Ignoring the questions regarding her disappearance, head high, she stuck to safer ground.

"Naturally I'll pay my share."

Not sure what else she ought to say, she played for time. Turning to Sean, she delicately raised a brow, but he, always the quiet one, simply smiled and pretended interest in the high, white clouds gathering to the east behind the ranges. Left holding the conversational bag, Kat changed the subject.

"The second coffin. Who was Therese?"

A muffled sob from one of the younger children made her regret her bluntness, but it was too late now.

With a huffing sniff, Bridget, glancing behind her at the gaggle of kids, dropped the hostilities.

"Dad married again, a bit after you left, Kat. Therese tried, but in the end, he dragged her down with him. Fill you in later. It's time we made a move to get out to the cemetery for the interment."

As one, they crossed to the last few cars in the carpark and headed out. Kat, still on her own, brought up the rear. Looked as if Colin Murphy didn't rate a ceremonial cortege through town. No big surprise there. The surprise lay in the number of people who'd actually bothered to turn out for him at all. Kat shrugged. It was no use jumping to conclusions with insufficient information. She'd just have to wait for introductions to the horde of new family members who had to be a mish-mash of in-laws, nieces, nephews, and, possibly half-siblings? The 'little ones' Marge had referred to?

~~~~~

Only eight chairs had been set ready in the grave-side front row, and all were occupied by her siblings and several children. Kat, still trailing behind, stepped back into the crowd, only to have a burly, grey-haired man in the second row swing his chair into the front and steer her into it. Startled, Kat looked more closely.

"John?"

Could this be Bridget's husband? John Hatton, with grey hair and a paunch?
~~~~~

A second, closer look assured her it really was him. Older, greyer, but still with the endearing twinkle she remembered in his deep-set blue eyes.

"Thanks," she said, smiling for the first time since arriving in The Crossing. She'd always liked John. When Colin tried to suck Bridget back to take care of the family when their mother, Monica, died, John had stood up to him, insisting he and Bridget go ahead with their marriage plans. Only ten at the time, she'd missed Bridget something fierce, but had silently admired John's refusal to let himself be browbeaten.

Once again, the officiating priest frowned Kat into silence. Mouth thinning, she frowned right back at him, slipping her sunglasses on, for privacy more than protection from the glare. Today was the first time in years she'd set foot in a church, and if this disapproving custodian was typical of modern church-men, she wouldn't be in a hurry to make another foray. Defiantly, she held her bare head high.

Bored with the drawn-out proceedings, Kat slowly surveyed the crowd. A few sort-of familiar faces she lingered on, then passed over. Eighteen years was a long time, but she was sure she'd identified Eddie Turner and a posse of her supporters. Her eyes tracked further, out to the edge of the modest gathering, meshing with those of a dark-haired man staring straight back at her from under the wide brim of a battered Akubra.

Her gut clenched. Her breath hitched in her throat. She felt herself drowning in his eyes, and, for a long moment, couldn't tear her gaze away.

Who in Hell is he?

Why is he staring at me?

Anyone else would have politely looked away as soon as she caught their eye, so why didn't he?

And why was she reacting to him like this? Sweat beaded her brow, but since it was actually rather cool, enough so to make her glad of her leather jacket, it wasn't down to the warmth of the day. She recognised the signs of burgeoning arousal. Of course she did, only she'd given up on men. Hadn't she?

Sean, sitting next to her, joggled her elbow, urging her to her feet to file past the grave and toss in the obligatory handful of dirt.

Distracted, she'd completely missed seeing her father, and the step-mother she'd never met, lowered into their graves. Standing within the shelter of her family, receiving the commiserations murmured by rote as the assembled mourners paid their respects, Kat boldly looked over her shoulder to where the bothersome man had been standing.

Was still standing.

And, her stomach lurched, a shiver feathering a path up her spine, was still staring at her. While she watched, her new-found brother, Mickey, Bridget had called him in her lightning introductions earlier, ran up to him. He turned to speak to the teenage boy, releasing her trapped gaze.

Who in Hell is he?

Kat had very definitely never seen that man before in her life.

If she had, she'd have remembered him! That she knew for certain.

2

Taking another sip from the cup of over-steeped tea Eddie Turner had thrust into her hand with a murmured word of condolence, Kat listened with half an ear as old Mrs Elliot waffled on, reminiscing on the days when she had gone to school with Colin Murphy.

"Such a handsome boy he was, dear. I remember dear Monica, too, Kathleen. Your mother's death was a dreadful tragedy. Dreadful. Now this. Those poor children, losing both parents, and them so young still."

The chime of a teaspoon tapping a cup, brought Mrs Elliot's rambling discourse to an end, to Kat's relief. Turning with everyone else in the CWA Hall where Bridget had arranged for morning tea to be served after the funeral, she watched her brother Patrick tug at his tie and clear his throat.

"Can I just say a few words, please?" Keeping it brief, Pat went on to thank people for attending and thank the CWA ladies for the spread they'd provided. "It's been good catching up, though, as I'm sure you realise, Dad and Therese's funerals aren't the reason I would have chosen to visit with you," he concluded.

"Now, if you don't mind, we'll say thank you and farewell. The family have been requested to meet with James Pritchard down at his office." Gathering the assorted Murphys with his eyes, he led the way from the hall.

~~~~~

Trailing behind once again, Kat squeezed into the conference room where chairs had been arranged facing a table at one end. James Pritchard, the town lawyer whom Kat remembered as a much younger man, and a plump woman she had noticed earlier sat waiting.

Opening with his condolences, Mr Pritchard introduced the woman at his side as Ms Annette Stubbins, a case worker who'd been appointed to the Murphy family some years earlier, then continued.

"Bridget," he nodded to her, "asked me to check for a will. Sorry to say, neither Colin nor Therese made a will. Not that either of them had anything to leave. I've taken care of what little paperwork their deaths entailed, and there's only one thing left to be settled."

He paused, looking from Bridget and John to Patrick and his wife, Karen, and finally, Sean, who were all seated in the front row. He bypassed Kat entirely. "Guardianship of their five minor children," he concluded.

At this point Ms Stubbins took over.

"Essentially," she said, her gaze also directed at the front row, "there are only two options. Either the children are placed with family members, which is usually our preferred solution, or they are taken into care and placed with foster families."
~~~~~

From her place in the back corner, Kat saw the children reach out to each other, joining hands. More than one of them sniffed back incipient tears.

Bridget, her voice heavy, spoke up.

"Ms Stubbins. Mr Pritchard. I discussed this with my brothers earlier, before we left for the church. Pat and Karen, John and I, are all farmers with other children of our own. This prolonged drought has knocked us about financially, and unfortunately, neither of us can take in the whole five, much as we'd like to. Sean," she nodded to him, "runs a hotel with his partner, and lives on the premises. We don't consider that a suitable environment for young children, especially the girls."

A tear trickled down her cheek, and her husband lay a sympathetic arm around her shoulders, hugging her close.

"What Bridget is saying," Pat chipped in, "is that Karen and I have agreed to take Ailsa and Dennis. Bridget and John will take the twins, Clarice and Estelle, and Micky will go to live with Sean and Robert."

"Is … is there no way we can stay together?" Ailsa choked out through her tears. At twelve years old she was way too young to shoulder responsibility for her siblings, but she took the lead anyway.

"You're all being really generous," fourteen-year-old Mickey, the picture of misery, backed up his sister. "But we're a family. We're all really close. I guess we'd hoped there'd be some way we wouldn't be split up."

"Oh, kids. I'm so sorry." Now Bridget was sobbing along with her much younger sisters. "We simply can't manage it."

Karen pulled a handkerchief from her purse and blew her nose, and Sean knuckled moisture from his eyes.

For a very long moment no-body spoke.

"I can take them. All five. I can keep them together."

Suddenly the focus of everyone's attention, Kat felt panic rising within her chest.

Bloody Hell! Where did that come from? She wished she could take the words back. Realised she couldn't.

"Kat?" Patrick found his voice first, before the others broke out in a babble of questions.

"Are you sure?"

No, I'm not sure. Not sure at all.

"Do you know what you'd be taking on?"

I haven't a bloody clue.

"Do you mean it? Can we really all come and live with you? Together?" Dennis, the closest child to where Kat sat in her corner, came and stood in front of her, staring at her from eyes which matched exactly those she saw every day in her mirror. Then his sisters joined him. Staring at her. Trusting her?

Finally, Mickey choked out, "Don't say things like that unless you mean them." His voice went from gruff to a cracked squeak, fierceness imbuing every word.

Kat stared back at them.

All five continued to eye her with mingled hope and fear.

"I mean it."

How could she even think of reneging with that battery of eyes boring into her. Even though the very thought of a pack of kids scared her to death.

3

The ensuing discussion, argument really, went on and on until Kat felt she'd scream if they didn't stop.

When she deemed everyone had had their say, Annette Stubbins clapped for attention.

"We've not been formally introduced," she began, smiling stiffly at Kat, "however I gather you're also one of Colin Murphy's children from his first marriage. Another sister to these children."

She looked down at the notes she'd been taking.

"Yes, Ms Stubbins. I'm Kathleen. Kat. The youngest of the four of us."

"Tell me about yourself, Kathleen Murphy, and why you should be considered as a suitable guardian. Do you have a partner who needs to be consulted? Where do you live? Can you support these children? How do you earn a living?"

"Apart from my being a sibling with the same rights and duty to family as Bridget, Patrick and Sean?"

Disgruntled at the third-degree treatment, Kat acknowledged that as she was an unknown quantity, the woman was entirely within her rights to demand to know more about her.

"I've recently returned to Australia from the United States, and to answer your questions; first, I'm entirely single, no children. Second and third, currently unemployed and homeless. Temporarily. I'm a doctor, looking to practise as a GP in a rural town. I'm told there's a shortage of doctors away from the coastal cities, so I don't anticipate any difficulties finding a place. After which I'll arrange housing, schools, etcetera."

"Doctor! Bloody Hell, Kat. That's what you always wanted. You've done well for yourself."

"I have, Sean, but it didn't just happen. It took a lot of hard work and determination. Ms Stubbins, I can provide references if you need them."

"We'll get to that in good time. As a doctor, I imagine you'll be able to cope financially with the extra burden five children will impose, but country GPs tend to get called out at all hours of the night and day. With no partner to pick up the slack, what will happen to the children then? They're too young to be left to their own devices."

Kat studied the five newly anxious faces in front of her.

"You're right, Ms Stubbins, they are. I guess a live-in housekeeper might be the best solution. I'll look into it when I find a place to live."

"You can live here."

"Yes!" "Yes!" several young voices exclaimed in unison.

"Yes, that's right, Kat. Oxley Crossing needs a new doctor."

"Then we won't have to leave our friends."

"The kids are right. The Crossing does need a doctor, and it's our home. We've all got friends here. Good friends, Kat. Can we stay in Oxley Crossing? Please?" Ailsa begged.

"Please?"

The barrage of youthful voices flustered Kat as her adult sibs and Annette Stubbins hadn't. Stay in The Crossing, though?

No way! Only, how to explain her antipathy? These children didn't know what they were asking.

"No. No, I don't think that will work, kids," she temporised. "I'm sure whoever's in charge will already have someone lined up to be doctor here. They won't want me."

"Actually, Dr Murphy," James Pritchard entered the conversation, "I happen to know there isn't anyone else in the offing. If you're properly qualified, I can't see anyone raising an objection to you taking over Doc Roberts's practice."

"Doc Roberts?" Kat had vague memories of a married man with several children younger than herself.

"What happened to him?"

"He had a stroke and was forced into retirement. The Crossing has been making do with a succession of locums for the last three months. When we can get them. If we don't find a permanent doctor soon, we'll lose our hospital. And the medical centre. It'll knock the stuffing out of the town."

James took off his glasses, polishing them on a pristine white handkerchief, not taking his eyes off Kat.

"Think it over, Dr Murphy. This is a good town, and the council is offering very generous incentives to professional people setting up here. Especially medical professionals. I suggest you go to see Bill Whitman down at the Council Office, and take your CV along for him to give it the once-over."

"See, Kattie. I told you."

Kattie?

Kat, feeling herself being backed into a metaphorical corner, glared at Dennis.

"It's Kat, little brother. I'll think it over, Mr Pritchard."

Soon after that the meeting came to an end. Kat walked out, the newly appointed guardian to five children.

"Oh, Kat, it's such a relief," Bridget sobbed, wrapping her sister in a constrictor-like hug. "We really didn't know how we'd cope. Now the kids can stay together as a family, here in The Crossing with all their friends. It's a good thing you're doing, and you can count on me to help any way I can."

"Us too," Pat seconded, speaking for both himself and Sean. "Any time you need us, Kat."

"Good girl." Taciturn as ever, John Hatton patted her on the shoulder, then, looking around at the Murphy clan congregated on the footpath, moved them on with a plaintive suggestion.

"Bridget, isn't it about time for lunch? Let's head over to *The Victoria*."

"I want to ride with Kat." Dennis grabbed her hand, abandoning Sean's ute which he'd been assigned to earlier.

"Us too."

Clarice and Estelle were quick to follow his lead, all three jumping into the yellow RAV-4 Kat had bought in Sydney the week before.

"Kat," Dennis yelled. "Where are Ailsa and Mickey going to sit? There's no more room?"

~~~~~

No more room. There'd been plenty of room when it was just herself. Kat massaged her temples where she felt the pounding beginnings of a headache. She didn't have time to indulge in a headache, even though thoughts of a dark, quiet room, all on her own, were incredibly tempting.

It was one thing to step up and say she'd take the children, but the reality was something else. Kat had to start thinking big. House, as well as car. Wherever they ended up, she had to accommodate herself, five kids and a housekeeper; and the days of the hired help living in poky attic rooms were long gone. A live-in housekeeper would expect proper staff quarters, something Australian houses didn't usually run to.

For the moment, no-one was paying Kat any attention and she let her mind replay the last hour.

She supposed if she was going to take on the job, she needed to give serious consideration to what was important to the kids and not simply demand they accept her dictates.

It was their life too.

They were entitled to a say. She had no intention of riding roughshod over them the way her father had over her.
~~~~~

Which might mean revising her attitude to The Crossing. She grimaced to herself. After the discussion in James Pritchard's office, she'd have to at least go through the motions of taking on Doc Roberts's practice or lose face with the whole family.

Well, no time like the present!

Pulling a notebook and pen out of her bag, she took a sip of the mineral water she'd ordered and began making a list, the process oddly calming. With a list she'd see clearly where she stood. With a list the big picture could be broken down into manageable chunks. With a list she might survive with her sanity intact.

Practice. Bill Whitman, Council.

Car.

House.

Housekeeper.

There. One step at a time. I can do with this.

"Whatcha doin' Kat?"

Dennis, of course. Even this early in their acquaintance Kat had Dennis pegged as the nosy one who could be relied on to trample willy-nilly over any tacit boundaries she set.

"Making plans, kiddo." She looked up, settling her gaze on John Hatton. "Any recommendations on a car to fit a family of six, John? Since I've been reliably informed my Rav-4 won't do." With a sly, sidelong glance, she poked Dennis with her foot, eliciting a giggle.

Several voices chipped in with suggestions, but Kat waited for John to answer.

"There's six of us," he said in his deliberate manner, "and we fit okay in our Honda Odyssey. Price is comparable with all those others. It handles well. Economical. Reasonable luggage space. Yeah, I reckon it'd do for you and the kids, Kat, but don't just take my word for it. There are other makes you might like to consider."

"True, but I reckon I can trust your recommendation, John." Their meals hadn't arrived yet, so Kat whipped her phone out and began tapping her way through the Honda website until she reached a salesman.

"Look, Mr Williams," she interrupted, "I don't need a spiel. I know what I want. A Honda Odyssey. Do you have one I can drive away immediately?" She listened to the reply. "Right. You've got a silver Odyssey in the showroom. Put my name on it, and I'll pick it up, … let's see. Wednesday morning? Can you have it ready to drive away soon as you open? Good. Guess you'd like a deposit."

She pulled out her debit card, and, in less than five minutes she'd bought a new car. With a small flourish, she ticked it off on her list as Marge Morris rolled out a trolley laden with plates of lamb roast with all the trimmings.

"Impressive, Kat." Murmured Sean who was seated next to her. "What's the encore? A house in ten minutes?"

Kat's lips twitched. "Could do, if I knew what I wanted. And where. I'm starving," she said, changing the subject. She wasn't prepared for discussions touching on her bank balance, and that was where this exchange was likely heading. "Let's eat."

~~~~~

"So, what's everyone doing now?"
~~~~~

Lunch over, they halted in the carpark to discuss the next move.

"Don't know about you guys, but if we're not needed, Karen and I are going to hit the road. We'd like to get home to our kids before too late."

"Yeah, you head off, Pat." Sean slapped his brother on the shoulder. "You too, Bridget. You've been holding the fort since Friday. Your kids will be missing you. If it's okay with everyone, I'll stay on for a couple of days and give Kat a hand getting sorted."

"Thanks everyone," Kat murmured, hugging Bridget, Pat and their families goodbye. "I'll stay in touch. I promise."

"We'll hold you to that, girl. No more disappearing into the blue without a word for eighteen years."

With Bridget and Sean driving the children back to the house and Pat already on the road to Glen Innes, Kat was left alone to pursue the remaining items on her steadily lengthening list.

"Take your time," Sean yelled, leaning out the window of his ute. "I'll take care of dinner."

4

"Whew! I'm bushed." Kat threw her keys and bag onto the table and flopped into a chair at the kitchen table.

"So, how much did you get done?" Sean laughed, the five kids avidly listening in despite the tele blaring in the background.

"Pretty much everything, and then some."

As Kat had intended, that wiped the grin of her smart-aleck brother's face. She reckoned he'd be treating her with a bit more respect shortly.

Sean turned the heat down under whatever he was making for dinner and sprawled in the chair opposite.

"C'mon. Tell all."

Determined not to be left out, the children quietly sidled in and claimed the empty chairs.

"Well, let's see." Although her stomach roiled just thinking of the dread future looming over her, elation at her afternoon's achievements meant Kat could barely keep a straight face.

"First stop was Hackett's Real Estate to sort out the rent on this place. We don't want to be evicted before we're ready to walk." She interrupted herself at this point with a digression.

"Boy, does the bush telegraph work well or not? Maree Hackett knew exactly who I was, assumed there was no question I'll be staying on as the local doctor, and had a property lined up to show me."

"Bit presumptuous, wasn't she?"

"Good saleswoman, more like. She assured me there really is only one house for sale in The Crossing with room for a live-in housekeeper and all of us. Nothing at all for rent."

"She knew about the housekeeper, too? That had to be Pritchard shooting his mouth off. I thought lawyers knew better than to discuss their client's business."

"Well, technically I'm not his client. I must have looked a bit surprised, because Maree told me confidentially, James Pritchard is on the medical recruitment committee who get to vet applicants, and in talking to her, was simply doing his bit to help me get settled."

"Reckon he's made his mind up you're staying. Who else is on this bloody committee, or is it a one-man-band?"

Kat ticked the names off on her fingers.

"James Pritchard, Bill Whitman from Council, Mike Patterson. Isn't he the bloke from the garage?"

"Yeah, he is," Mickey affirmed. "He's an okay guy."

Kat nodded.

"Then there's someone called Frances Porteus, whom I gather is Director of Nursing at the hospital, and last, but certainly not least, Barbara Morgan. Alan's mum I think."

"That's right. She's Melanie's Grandma."

Kat smiled encouragingly at Ailsa, glad to hear her sister sounding more confident. It bothered her that the kids, including Dennis, despite appearances to the contrary, seemed to be so cowed. Scared to stand up for themselves. She didn't like it. She reckoned the Old Man must have been as free with a backhander with them as he had been with Sean and herself. Her lips tightened. That bastard had a lot to answer for.

"Anyway," she forced the smile back on her face. "Back to my afternoon. Maree described the house, it's Doc Roberts's place, by the way, right across the street from the hospital, and it sounded pretty good. I made it clear a sale was contingent on my taking on the practice, and that I'd want immediate occupancy. She didn't turn a hair. Said she'd phone Doc about it. She also suggested I talk to Eddie Turner ... Patterson," she corrected herself, "regarding a housekeeper. Seems she knows everyone."

"Hell, Kat. I was only joking about you buying a house as well as the car."

"I know, but we have to live somewhere. It's not bought yet, although I had Maree show me around after I'd finished up at Council. That's why I'm so late. Anyway, acting on her advice, I stopped off at the library. Eddie was really helpful. She not only thinks she knows someone who might like the housekeeping job, but she helped me customise my CV and write a cover letter to go with it, for the committee. We emailed it straight off to all the committee members, then I went over to talk to Bill Whitman."

Kat grinned, enjoying recounting her eventful afternoon.

"It was pretty obvious both he and Eddie had also been given a heads-up before I arrived. So that's where I'm up to. Now I wait on Council getting back to me before I can do any more."

To Kat, it felt like a conspiracy. Oxley Crossing was ganging up on her. Trapping her. She could feel her escape route closing by the minute.

"In that case, we might as well have dinner."

The words had scarcely left Sean's mouth when Kat's phone rang, and her chances of escape narrowed still further.

"Dr Murphy speaking," she answered, stepping out onto the rickety back veranda for a modicum of privacy. Ten minutes later she returned to the kitchen, and the dinner which had been held back, waiting for her.

Taking pity on the poorly contained curiosity surrounding her, she relented.

"That was a Mrs Margaret Bardon. Seems Eddie came good. Maggie Bardon is applying for the job of doctor's housekeeper. We're having lunch tomorrow to see if we suit each other."

"That was quick work!"

"Yeah. But why wait? I guess The Crossing really wants me. Surprising as that feels." And it did.

Sean's excellent shepherd's pie sat heavy in Kat's stomach. Hoping she'd be found wanting, and therefore free to put Oxley Crossing in her rear-view mirror forever, she had gone through the motions, only to find herself caught.

She'd downplayed her interview with Bill Whitman, but he too had spoken as if committee approval was a foregone conclusion, when, if she'd been consulted, she would have put herself at the bottom of their list. With a black line drawn through her name.

Without hesitation.

Feeling sorry for herself, Kat let the children's muted chatter wash over her.

Dinner over, Mickey and Ailsa tackled the washing up while Sean put the kettle on for a cuppa. Kat, as an excuse to grab a few minutes to herself, took her overnight bag through to the bedroom. The master bedroom. The only spare space in this pokey dump. If she'd thought it would work, she'd have offered to swap it for Sean's swag on floor of the lounge. Apparently, Bridget had been sleeping here, and had put clean sheets on for her before she left. Something to be thankful for. A tentative investigation revealed the springs were gone leaving the mattress sagging in the middle. Kat sniffed, anticipating an uncomfortable night.

"Anyone home?" A knock rattled the front door simultaneously with the enquiry.

"Charlie!" Mickey tossed the dish towel to Dennis and went to welcome the visitor. "Come in."

"My condolences, kids. Sorry to intrude," their visitor flicked a glance towards Sean.

"Thought I'd better check in with Mickey."

"With Mick? What for, Mate?"

Standing in the shadowed doorway, Kat, recognition setting her nerves jangling, silently seconded her brother's blunt question.

Disgruntled, she studied their visitor, trying to figure out why this bloke who'd caught her eye during the interment had made such an impact. Tall, with thick, brown curls badly in need of a trim, wary coffee-dark eyes and what she grudgingly conceded to be ruggedly attractive features, he was far removed from what she usually considered 'her type'. Besides, he'd already talked to Mickey. Why did he think he had the right to come barging in uninvited?

"Oh, sorry mate. Charlie Reynolds, Oxley Crossing Nursery. Mickey works for me on weekends. Or used to."

"Yeah. About that, Charlie, I'll be there as usual, this weekend," Mickey said, then thought again. "Unless … Kat?" Tense and uncertain, he turned to look at her.

"You'd better come in." Kat stepped into view. "Tea or coffee, Charlie Reynolds?"

Their visitor hesitated, but Mickey urged him forward.

"Come in and meet Sean and Kat. They're our brother and sister."

Claiming the initiative, Kat held out her hand. Then wished she hadn't when his touch generated an unwelcome heat. In the bustle to find seats at the table, she surreptitiously wiped her hand on her jeans. For all the good that did. Her palm still tingled. She didn't like the way her hormones sat up and took notice of Charlie Reynolds.

He was a complication she could do without.

"Here, sit down." Sean pulled a chair out and plonked a trio of steaming mugs on the table.

"This job of Mickey's," Kat asked, dispensing with social pleasantries, intent on moving their guest on and out as quickly as possible. "What's it entail? I'm Mickey's guardian, in case you're wondering what business it is of mine."

"Oh. I thought he was going with Sean? I've been hearing all sorts of wild stories down the pub. Which is why I dropped in. I thought, if there's a chance Mickey's staying put, I don't want to give his job away to someone else."

"Nah, Mate. Change of plans. Instead of splitting the kids up, Kat's taking on the whole pack." Sean grinned.

"What? All of them?" Charlie swung back to Kat who was still waiting on an answer. It took him a moment to get his mind back to her question.

"Right. Mickey's job. Saturdays and an occasional Sunday. Nothing too involved. Mick helps me get shipments ready to go out Monday morning to the retailers. Maybe does a bit of propagating or weeding if there's time."

"That's right, Kat." Mickey stated, eager for her approval. "I wanted to start saving up to pay my way through uni. I mow lawns and do gardening for some of the oldies around town, too, after school. What's going to happen? I need to tell them if you say I can't do it anymore."

"Okay."

Kat sipped tea strong enough to stand a spoon in, mentally making a note to acquire some of the delicate herbal infusions she preferred.

"Unless I discover you're an unsuitable influence, Charlie Reynolds, I see no reason to ban Mick's working for you. I can't see us moving from The Crossing before next week, so we'll leave things as they are for the time being and ..."

"Moving! But you promised we could stay. You're going to be the doctor and we can stay here with our friends. You promised!"

"Ailsa, I thought you understood. That promise is conditional on ..."

The opening bars of Beethoven's Ninth interrupted Kat's explanation. With a quick frown at the screen, she was on her feet and retreating to the veranda once more.

"Hang fire, everyone. This is Bill Whitman."

Sean drifted over to the door behind her, hanging back till she finished talking.

"Doctor?" Charlie, marooned at the table, looked at the worried faces of the children gathered around him, wishing someone would fill him in on Kat Murphy. He found the woman disturbing in ways he'd prefer not to think about.

"Yeah. Kat's a doctor," Dennis, proud as punch, proclaimed.

"She said she'd take over from Doc Roberts," Ailsa wailed, "and now she's talking about moving somewhere else."

"It wasn't settled, remember," Mickey, equally worried, cautioned his sister. "You heard what she told Sean. It depends on the committee approving her application."

"But ... she's a doctor, and the town needs her. I thought ..." Ailsa pulled a crumpled tissue from her pocket and dabbed at her eyes.

For the next ten minutes, they made desultory conversation, pretending they weren't all waiting for Kat. Charlie, his coffee mug empty, wondered whether he oughtn't to make tracks.

"Mick, let me know what's going on, Mate." Half-way to the door, he halted when Kat returned, stopping for a few quietly murmured words with Sean on the way in.

"Bad news, Sis?" Had to be, judging by her downturned mouth and slumped shoulders. He wished he could make everything right for her. Guilt had been gnawing at him all afternoon. Years ago, he'd let his little sister down badly when he lit out on his own, leaving her, a thirteen-year-old kid, to cope with their father's drinking and worsening violent mood-swings on her own.

"Depends on your point of view. Seems I'm in. No escape now."

No escape? He gaped at her. Had he read the situation all wrong? Didn't she want the job?

"Can't you just refuse if you don't want it?"

"You heard Ailsa. I promised."

"Do you really hate the place that much?"

"Oh, I suppose it's not the town so much as all the bad memories, although it did feel good this afternoon, flaunting my success in their faces. The good-for-nothing daughter of the town drunk who's made something of herself in spite of what they predicted."

Sean winced at the bitterness in her voice. He'd heard rumours, but, bloody hell … Had it been worse than he'd thought? Guilt gnawed at his conscience.

"They value me now, though, don't they?" Kat thought a moment, then added, "Actually, with the incentives Council are throwing in, this could be my dream practice. Anywhere else and I'd be over the moon. Stupid, huh?"

Not waiting for an answer, she strode over to the table and reclaimed her chair.

"Okay. Listen up people. That was Bill Whitman. The committee held an emergency meeting over dinner. According to Bill, they were all impressed no end with my qualifications and voted unanimously to approve my application. You're looking at Dr Kathleen Murphy, permanent full-time GP in Oxley Crossing as from next Monday."

"In one afternoon? The same Shire Council that held up my development application for three months because someone was on long-service leave? Lucky you." Charlie shook his head.

"Guess doctor trumps nurseryman," Kat smirked.

It took another second for the kids to grasp what had happened, then chaos broke out until Sean banged on the table for silence.

"Congratulations, Sis. If I had a bottle of champers handy, I'd drink to your success."

"Does that mean we stay here?" Estelle tugged on Kat's sleeve.

"Yeah, I guess it does, Estelle. Not in this house, though." Kat barely suppressed a shudder. "It's too small for us and a housekeeper. We'll be moving into Doc Roberts's place as soon as I can arrange it." The happy smiles greeting her announcement eased the heaviness in her heart.

"Mickey, you're free to go on working for Charlie and your oldies. Now, if you all don't mind, I've got some more phone calls to make."

It seemed mere moments till Charlie Reynolds was gone, the kids off to bed, and just Sean and Kat left in the kitchen. Kat finished texting an update to Maggie Bardon, then another to Maree Hackett, telling her to prepare the house contract for signing.

"Done! God, Sean, I'm just about dead on my feet. It's been one hell of a day, but at least it's all downhill from here. Just a few contracts to sign tomorrow and I'm done."

"You're bloody amazing, Kat. If I hadn't seen you in action myself, I'd never have believed anyone could completely turn their life inside out and upside down so completely in one afternoon. I was wondering, though," he sneaked a sidelong glance, "in all the kerfuffle, you never did say what brought you back to The Crossing at the exact moment we all needed you."

Kat considered telling him to mind his own business, then shrugged. She supposed it was his business. Sort of.

"For my birthday last year, my colleagues in San Francisco gave me an arrangement of Australian wildflowers. I had a bit of a homesick meltdown. Did some thinking and made plans to come back. To Australia, not specifically The Crossing. That bit was down to my friend, Helga Lundstrom, a psychologist. She'd been helping me work through a few issues after the divorce. Told me I ought to sort out my ancient hang-ups with family and this place. Decided to start with Dad, then move on."

That was the short version. Kat saw no need to elaborate on the handful of basic facts.

"You didn't mention you were married."

"Divorced. Marriage was one huge mistake." One she had no intention of discussing with Sean. Or anyone else, for that matter.

Her brother gave her one of his piercing stares, then shrugged, letting it go. He moved on to her mention of family.

"Seems to me, any issues you had with family are water under the bridge after today."

"Yeah. Guess so. As for Oxley Crossing, my bad memories were down to people's attitudes more than the place itself. A lot of them have probably moved on. Those that haven't, I'll deal with, I suppose. I'll have to, won't I? I'm turning in, Sean. Tomorrow's going to be another busy day, following up on today's groundwork. Bill wants to see me bright and early. At least everything's in train. After tomorrow I'll put my feet up till I have to open the surgery."

"Sounds good to me." Sean yawned and went to unroll his swag. Suddenly he swung back to his sister.

"Hey, Kat. Give me a squiz at that list of yours. Something I want to check."

Yawning, Kat pulled the notebook from her bag and handed it to him, open at the list with every item ticked off, some with notes appended.

"What's the problem? I've dealt with everything."

"Maybe not. Does Doc's house come furnished? 'Cause if it doesn't, you're going to have to buy furniture. Assuming you don't want this junk."

He waved a disparaging hand, indicating their father's scabby, mismatched furnishings.

Appalled, Kat stared at him. No way was she taking this rubbish with her.

"Hell, Sean. It completely slipped my mind." She sat down with a thump, feeling the chair move uneasily beneath her. "I'll have to buy *everything*. The whole house, top to bottom, for seven people." She turned to a clean page, heading it with the one word – FURNITURE.

When's it going to end?

Abruptly, she tossed the pen down and stood up.

"Tomorrow. I'm going to bed. I'll deal with this tomorrow."

5

Tuesday the sun shone out of a cloudless sky and Oxley Crossing, clean, bright and welcoming as Kat did not remember it from the past, looked like an ad for a tree-change.

Yeah, she supposed, *the place is probably okay, but, the people …?* She'd hold fire on that one. *Although, … the kids seemed pretty happy. Reckoned they had friends worth sticking around for. Unlike me.*

Murphys as valued members of the community was so not the way she remembered it. She recalled being picked on because her father ended up in drunken fights on Saturday nights, with her mother having to go and bring him home. And their social standing had gone all the way downhill after a burst aneurism brought a premature end to her mother's life.

I'll see.

All this gratuitous welcoming friendliness made her edgy and suspicious. What if, when the news got out, popular opinion gave her the thumbs down? It wasn't as if anyone except Fred and Izzy had gone out of their way for her in the past.

Now the civic leaders were falling over themselves to recruit her. To help her settle in.

Amazing what a few framed degrees hanging on the wall can do for a person's public image.

She wondered how long it would take for the whispers to begin circulating. Then she'd see just how badly they wanted a doctor.

Too bad. They're stuck with me now. I've given my word.

Maree Hackett opened at eight-thirty, so Kat began there, signing the contract to buy her house. Committing herself to a future in Oxley Crossing. The last place she'd ever imagined living.

"What did Doc say about immediate occupancy? It's going to make things difficult if he doesn't agree."

"I couldn't get onto him last night. I'll try again now."

The call was picked up in seconds, and the approval given.

"Hang on a minute. Let me talk to him." Kat reached for the phone. "Doctor Roberts? Kat Murphy. Thanks for agreeing to let us in. It'll make my life so much easier if I can get the kids settled before I start work. Just one other thing, though. Do you mind if I make a head-start on the gardens without waiting till all the paperwork's filed? I've got a few ideas for landscaping, and this is a good time of the year to plant stuff."

"You're not going to grub out my roses, are you?" An alarmed feminine voice broke in.

"My wife. I'm on speaker," Doc grunted. "Loves those bloody rose bushes."

"Not to worry, Mrs Roberts. I was thinking more of putting in some fruit trees and vegetables out the back." Kat crossed mental fingers. The roses would be going from their prime position lining the front footpath, but she did like their perfume. Maybe she'd put them in pots. Give them a second chance. Then she wouldn't technically be lying.

"That's alright, then." Mrs Roberts again. "If you need any help with my roses, talk to Eddie. She's an expert."

Sounds like Eddie's become quite the go-to person.

It wasn't the way Kat remembered *her* either, although she had to admit Eddie Turner had been a good organiser.

And less judgemental than most.

The conversation concluded amicably a few exchanges later, by which time the Council office was open and Kat signed a few more contracts in Bill Whitman's office.

"Goodo. All done. I was afraid we weren't going to find a new doctor."

Kat thought the shire president was going to kiss her, he was so happy, and, not being much of a touchy-feely person, smartly stepped back to hand-shaking range.

"Brenda," he called his secretary in, "take Dr Murphy up to the Medical Centre and introduce her to Nancy Perdis. She's the office manager," he explained.

"You'll have no troubles with Nancy, Doctor, or anyone else for that matter. We're all over the moon to have you on board."

He was right. Nancy was another one overjoyed to meet her. Many more and she might believe in her welcome.

"Thank the Good Lord we've finally got someone," Nancy exclaimed, ushering Kat through the waiting room into what would now be her office and examining room.

"'Ere, Nance. Is that this doctor I've been hearing so much about? Gettin' ta see 'er, am I?"

"Yes she is, and no, Tom Carey, you aren't," Nancy replied to the elderly patient waiting to see the practice nurse. "Nurse Macintosh will be with you shortly."

Kat stopped, looking back over her shoulder.

"Tom Carey? Is that really you? How are you?" Hand out in welcome, she bent down to the old chap. He had to be pushing ninety, she estimated. He'd been newly retired when she left town.

"Heh, heh. Ya see, Nance. The doc knows me already. You always were a good girl, Kat Murphy. Always knew you'd do well for yerself."

"Wasn't what you said when I patched you up that time you came off your bike. How are you, Tom? And your mate. Matt Hendersen?"

"Kickin' along. Orright most days, the both of us. No use complainin', is there? Hear you've taken on that pack of kids yer dad left. They'll be a hell of a lot better off with you, girlie."

Nancy sniffed impatiently in the background, reminding Kat this wasn't a social event.

"I'll see you around, Tom."

I'd forgotten about Tom and Matt, she mused, an unexpected warmth perking her up. She almost laughed aloud.

I had more well-wishers back in the day than I realised. Fred and Izzy Hayes, the crooked publicans, and a couple of old barflies. They wouldn't do much for her professional image, but, damn it all, Tom Carey was a friend. The first she'd encountered in The Crossing of today.

A wide grin lighting up her normally distant, shuttered expression, she followed Nancy into her very own sanctum.

Compact. Superbly equipped, just as Bill promised, Kat observed, running a possessive finger over the sleek body of a state-of-the-art computer waiting for her to boot it up.

"All our files are digital," Nancy commented. "We completed the conversion last year. Now, Doctor, if you'll just sign these forms, I'll get them in today's mail and you'll be legal to start work. You could even take afternoon surgery, if you like."

That was a bit short-noticed. Startled, Kat was about to answer sharply when she caught Nancy's sly grin and chuckled instead. No need to stir the possum.

"Not if I don't have to, Nancy. Was sort of counting on having this week free to get the kids settled. Unless you really need me?" She raised a brow. Just how desperate were they?

Nancy shook her head.

"Fair enough, I reckon. Barring emergencies we can hold it together till Monday. Now the paperwork is out of the way, come on through to the kitchen for a cuppa, Dr Murphy. Then I'll leave you to find your way around."

"Right. And Nancy? The name's Kat."

"Hi, I'm Fiona MacIntosh. Practice nurse." The newcomer who'd bustled in on their heels thrust out her hand.

"I've finished with Tom Carey, Nance. Time for a break before my next appointment. Boy, am I glad to see you, Dr Murphy. I've been treading on eggshells, trying to hold the practice together without a doctor."

"Glad to meet you," Kat got in with a handshake when Fiona slowed for a breath. "And the name's Kat. We'll have a good chat when you're not so busy."

"Guess what, Fi? Tom Carey's an old mate of Kat's. You should have seen him. Like a dog with two tails, he was."

Fiona MacIntosh lost her smile.

"That old sot? I'd advise you to steer clear of the likes of him, Kat. You don't want to go round stirring up unpleasant memories."

Bewildered, Nancy stared from Fiona to Kat. That sharp comment had been so unlike easy-going Fiona. She shivered. For a moment the bright, sunny kitchen felt more like a deep freeze.

There were still shards of ice edging Kat's mild words when she replied.

"Nah. Not happening. I don't turn my back on my friends. Especially not ones I owe as much to as Tom Carey and Matt Hendersen."

"What on earth would you owe that pair?"

Kat almost let it go at that.

Then didn't.

Sometimes a woman simply *had* to take a stand.

"You offered me a bit of free advice, Fiona, so I'll return the favour. Those unpleasant memories you mentioned? Mostly a pack of exaggerations and lies made up by people who were happy to turn their backs and do nothing while a violent drunk knocked his kids around."

Fiona's flush could have started a bushfire.

"I … I … I didn't mean anything Doctor. I just didn't want you being made to feel unwelcome, that's all. I don't believe what I heard. Not for a minute."

But you gave those old rumours enough credit to mention them.

Kat narrowed her eyes, but this time, in the interests of workplace harmony, kept her thoughts to herself.

"No hard feelings?" Kat, assuming a wary smile which didn't quite reach her eyes, offered her hand.

Slowly, Fiona reached out to accept it. Lifting her head to meet Kat's eyes, she nodded in tacit apology.

"Would someone please explain what's going on?"

"Sorry, Nancy." Kat let her shoulders slump, the tenseness draining away. "You weren't in Oxley Crossing eighteen years ago, were you? It was just a few old coals being raked over. Nothing to worry about." She turned back to Fiona MacIntosh. "Are you going to be able to work with me, Fiona?"

Fiona's flush, which had faded, bloomed anew.

"Yes," she snapped. Remembering how much she needed this job, she became more conciliatory.

"I only mentioned it because of what some people are saying. I didn't mean anything by it. Mum always said she didn't believe the half of what she heard back then. She taught you English, you know."

"I wondered. I always liked her. I thought her name was so pretty. Poppy. How is she?" Not in the same league as old Tom, still, Poppy MacIntosh had always treated her fairly.

"She tried to set Social Services on your father for the way he neglected you, you know, but Mr Hinch, the principal, refused to support her. Said you'd be finished school in a few months and not their problem any longer. Sounds like one of those back-turners you mentioned."

"There's a lot of them in the world," Kat commented. "I'm glad we'll be working together, Fiona," she concluded, giving the other woman the benefit of the doubt.

"Me too." Taking her coffee with her, Fiona went to greet her next patient.

<div style="text-align:center">~~~~~</div>

"Frances Porteus, Doctor. Director of Nursing." Matron Porteus, as the old-fashioned locals preferred to call her, ushered Kat into her office. "You'll be wanting to look over the hospital and the Steedman Wing. Our Aged Care Residential wing, you know. We have twelve beds for elderly locals who are too frail to be cared for in their own homes."

"I do, Ms Porteus. I'm so looking forward to attending here."

"We'll have a cuppa first, then I'll show you around."

Another cuppa. Her fourth since breakfast.

Any more and she'd be floating out the door on a flood of tea. Kat had forgotten how every meeting in country Australia was accompanied by an offer to put the kettle on, but it was a friendly custom, so she smiled and nodded agreeably.

With both women meeting each other more than half way, they were soon on good terms when Frances introduced a topic which, so soon after her unsettling confrontation with Fiona, set Kat's hackles rising.

"Kat, I must warn you, on my rounds this morning I heard quite a few hair-raising stories from our aged care residents. They'd heard about your appointment already, can you believe?"

Kat could. Easily. The Oxley Crossing bush telegraph was fully functioning, and faster than a post going viral on Facebook.

"Well, I dismissed their gossip in no uncertain manner. Eighteen years ago you were a child, and however precocious, would never have got up to a quarter of what they claimed."

Frances waved dismissively.

"Unfortunately, they're not going to be alone in their storytelling. We have to nip this in the bud, Kat. We can't have people maligning your reputation on the strength of a few apocryphal tall stories from the Dark Ages. You leave it to me. I'll have a word with Eddie Patterson. She'll know how best to handle it."

Really? Eddie again?

Kat took a moment to marshal her thoughts.

"Apocryphal the stories may be, Fran, but unfortunately there's a kernel of truth. Buried deep, but still …"

Surprising Kat, Fran actually chuckled.

"Usually is. This is the problem with coming back to your home town. I'm lucky none of this lot know what I got up to in my younger days."

Cups emptied, they set off on their tour in perfect charity with each other.

Maybe, if there are more as tolerant as Fran, life in The Crossing won't be too bad after all.

~~~~~

With time in hand before her meeting with Maggie Bardon, Kat wandered across the street to take another look at her house. Hers! One of the most prestigious addresses in Oxley Crossing, sprawled across a huge double block. Although, somehow, it didn't look very appealing to her. Not as she envisioned her home.

The house, while nothing special, architecturally speaking, was a generous family home. Then she realised what grated. The landscaping was lacklustre. Boring. Neat, tidy, narrow beds. Concrete central path in a straight line from mailbox to front door. Mrs Roberts's precious standard roses a soldierly straight line bordering the front footpath. And a bare expanse of lawn, already browning off as the weather warmed. Nothing intrinsically wrong, Kat shuddered. It was typical of thousands of similar front gardens across the country. But this one was *hers*. And it was very definitely not to her taste.

"Dr Kathleen. Surveying your domain?" Charlie wasn't sure why, but it just felt right, somehow, to use the new doc's proper given name. Warm and sweet-tasting in his mouth. Moreish.
~~~~~

Lost in her own thoughts, Kat jumped, the unexpected presence of the man standing way too close to her sending a jolt of female awareness slamming into her. She almost called him on using her full name, only … All those rounded vowels and extra long consonants had sounded … She wasn't sure exactly why, but she'd liked the sound of her name on his tongue. It had felt warm. Almost a caress. So different to the sneering tones of past detractors which had led to her shortening the Kathleen her mother had always used to the short, sharp Kat she answered to today. She could get to enjoy hearing her name if it always sounded like this. Not letting on, though, she turned slowly, subjecting the audacious man to a searching examination, not sure she liked the knowing grin on his face.

"Oh, it's you, Charlie Reynolds. I seem to be tripping over you every time I turn around."

Knowing she sounded truculent, she didn't care. She wasn't entirely happy that he aroused the sort of feelings which reduced her to a wary nervousness. This man might set her pulse racing; however, she had no interest in relationships. Although she had been known to scratch an itch now and then. Maybe …? Only, did she really want to set tongues wagging with new indiscretions? When nothing lasting could come of it?

"You were frowning. Something wrong?"

And why do I care, Charlie asked himself. He'd sworn off women since way before settling in The Crossing, turning the hobby farm inherited from his grandfather into a viable nursery business. He'd steadfastly resisted the old biddies with their matchmaking efforts, so why had he impulsively crossed the street for another squiz at the new doc?

He deliberately ignored how even the tiniest glimpse of her set his heart hammering in his chest.

"Wrong?" Kat waved a hand at her innocently offending garden. "You're supposed to be in the plant business, and you ask me what's wrong with that aesthetic wasteland masquerading as a garden?"

Why couldn't he simply turn and walk away? Every instinct Charlie possessed warned him Kat Murphy was dangerous to his peace of mind, but her appeal to his professional integrity was as irresistible as her appeal to his baser instincts.

Charlie's lips twitched. He felt similarly about most people's gardens. What surprised him was finding the new doc to be a like-minded soul.

"So, what grandiose plans are you hatching, Kathleen?"

And there it was again, that warmth curling deep in her belly. Seemed those who claimed names hold powerful magic were absolutely correct. Kat clamped down hard on her instinct to smile at him.

"Jeez, Reynolds. Give me a break. I only arrived in The Crossing yesterday. I've got no idea what to do about it. I simply know I can't live with it as it is."

"You know," Charlie tried to shut his mouth. He really did, only to have the unrestrained invitation come spewing out. "I'm a qualified landscaper. I'm already imagining several different possibilities. Call on me when you're ready. If you want."

"Yeah?"

About to brush him off, Kat changed her mind. This was The Crossing.

No way Charlie Reynolds would conveniently vanish, never to be seen again. The place for too small for that. If she let him into her life, in a strictly professional capacity of course, sooner or later she'd get over the disturbing effect he had on her libido. Aversion therapy. It worked wonders with allergies. Flustered by the turn her thoughts had taken, she rushed to find a distraction.

"Do you stock fruit trees?" Without waiting for an answer, she strode off down the drive, Charlie trailing along in her wake. "I was thinking I'd like to espalier fruit trees down both sides. Maximise the space." Wondering where her ideas were coming from, she waved her arms at the metre-wide strip of bare earth either side of the concrete driveway, almost clipping Charlie in the chest when he followed too closely. "Apples and pears one side of the driveway and stone fruits the other. Then," she darted into the back yard and pointed to the side of the free-standing shed. "Maybe citrus along here? What do you think? I want a fresh food garden with as many different kinds of edibles as will fit."

"Jeez, Murphy." Relieved to be distracted from the direction his thoughts had been edging towards, he tossed her paraphrased words back at her. "For someone with no idea you seem to know exactly what you want. I can sort out an espaliered orchard for you. No sweat. When do you want it?"

"This weekend?" He looked taken aback, but why should she wait? "It's the planting season, isn't it? I need to think about the front for a bit, but Doc Roberts gave me permission to put in some fruit and vegetables immediately."

Although what she was planning was probably a whole lot more than Doc Roberts had been thinking.

"I'll need to measure up. Make a list of what you need. Sort out what trees to use." Charlie whipped out his phone and began taking notes, checking details with Kat as he did so.

"Okay. I'll leave you to it. I've got somewhere else I need to be. See you."

Looking up, Charlie was startled to see Kat disappearing back out to the street. He shook his head. Kathleen Murphy was a hard woman to keep up with. They hadn't even mentioned a budget for the project. *Good reason to catch up with her again soon,* his sneaky inner voice whispered.

Charlie scowled. Maybe he'd hand this job over to his foreman. Even as he thought this, he knew he wouldn't. Sworn off women or not, Kat Murphy drew him inexorably deeper. He'd take care of her garden himself, damn it.

~~~~~

"Coffee?"

"No thanks. You can dunk one of these for me though." Kat tossed the pack of lemon and ginger teabags she'd bought that afternoon to her brother. "Something smells good."

"Yeah," Sean agreed. "Massaman curry for dinner, and I made Anzacs and chocolate slice for the kids."

"Hell, Sean. Why am I looking for a housekeeper?" she laughed. "I ought to sign you up. Keep it in the family."

"Reckon Rob might have something to say to that," he grinned, eyes sliding away from hers.

"Anyway, Sis, what'd ya get up to today?"
~~~~~

He was agog for the latest instalment. Watching his little sister's whirlwind assault on Oxley Crossing was the most entertainment he'd had since Mrs Wallace's pig got loose and wandered into Robert's bar last month. The old sow led them a merry chase. Robert reckoned it left the regulars so thirsty their pub showed the best mid-week profit all year. He wished Rob was here to see Kat in action. He'd get a real kick.

"Just about got it all wound up." She filled him in on her morning, concluding with an account of her lunch with Maggie Bardon.

"She seems like a winner, Sean. Won't know till I see her in action, however, I'm quietly optimistic. She gave me a few useful tips about tomorrow's big furniture shop, too. I've teed up a personal assistant at the biggest homewares store in Tamworth who'll walk me through the different departments and arrange delivery. On Friday, Sean."

Kat laughed.

"Tried to tell me it couldn't be done, until I threatened to go elsewhere. She came to the party then, alright. Money talks. Finished up with a swing by the school to make myself known and give them the new family details and contact numbers. That's a place that's changed, Sean. For the better, no question. Ben Wright's a vast improvement on Archie Hinch. Not hard, but still ... I was impressed."

Kat glanced around, frowning at the silence.

"Speaking of the kids, where have they disappeared to?"

"Mickey's doing someone's garden, and the others are in the park with their mates." He cast a glance at the clock.

"Due back anytime, then I've told them they have to do their homework before dinner. By the way, Kat. You might think I've overstepped, but I lined up a couple of handymen for you. You just need to tell them when you need them."

"Handymen?"

"Yeah. Unless you're a whizz with a set of allen keys and a screwdriver. We redid the pub a while back, and half the stuff was delivered in flatpacks. Assembly required."

Kat shuddered. Another potential stuff-up her brother had saved her from. Getting back together with him was good in more ways than one. She pulled out her phone and called the number on the slip of paper he handed her, booking Sam Gill and his brother Russell for Friday.

"I was down the shops today. You've really set this town back on its heels. You and your cavalier way with red tape is all everybody was talking about. They sounded proud of you, Kat."

He cast a sideways glance in her direction, tossing up whether or not to get personal. Then did.

"I know this wasn't what you wanted, Sis, but is it really so bad. The kids? The Crossing?"

He felt guilty at being a party to pushing her into it. Worried she might not cope long term.

Kat took her time answering.

Her first instinct had been to tell him to butt out, but she wasn't a prickly teenager any longer. That was genuine concern she read in her brother's face.

"No, I wasn't looking for it, any of it, that's true. But, you know, Sean? I had a choice. Several choices. I put my hand up for the kids when I didn't have to. You'd all got them sorted, only, I could see *they* weren't happy. Shocked myself as much as the rest of you. I don't regret taking them on. It won't be a bed of roses, though, that's for sure. Five kids, Sean. Five! I must be mad." She shook her head, a rare, quirky grin slowly spreading over her face.

"Don't regret it though, so stop worrying, will ya? The Crossing? That's harder to explain. I think part of it was giving the finger to those who put me down in the past and generally made my life hell. Funny thing is, the people who count today all seem to want me on board. They're bending over backwards to accommodate me. Reckon it won't hurt to give it a go here. I can always dump The Crossing and move on if it doesn't pan out."

Kat laughed at Sean's blatant scepticism.

"I was thinking earlier," Sean mused. "About what ifs. What if you hadn't arrived in time? What if Dad hadn't been such an arsehole? What if ..."

"We could go on forever asking 'What if?'," Kat interrupted, "and none of it changes a thing, does it? Waste of time."

"Although, you've got to admit, Kat, there are certain turning points, choices, that are more relevant than what shirt to wear to the office."

"True. Like me deciding to steal apples from Fred Hayes's tree at the back of the pub."

Kat laughed.

"When I got caught, and abused him and Izzy for letting Dad put all his pay over the bar instead of buying food for me, forcing me to steal so I could eat, they took me under their wing. The good citizens were scandalised by a thirteen-year-old girl working at the pub, but Fred and Izzy Hayes were the best thing that ever happened to me."

"You count the Hayes brothers as the best thing? Those two were so bloody crooked they made a dog's hind leg look straight!"

Sean looked so taken aback Kat laughed again.

"Sure. They looked out for me better than my own father ever did. Fed me. And paid me so I got to save some money for uni. They empowered me, Sean. Taught me to believe in myself. Izzy described me once as their redeeming good deed. They even fixed me up with a place to live and a job to pay my way through uni when I left town, you know. They were good friends, Sean. In spite of being on the shady side of the law more often than not. Unfortunately, people were scandalised and there was gossip."

She glanced up at him, wondering how much of it he'd heard.

"Bridget got to hear what was being said, which led to an almighty row. She never did learn that telling me what to do guaranteed I'd do the opposite. Hope she doesn't start on me again when she's over the shock of having me back."

She laughed again, and changed the subject.

"Reckon Helga would be right proud of me."

"Helga?"

"My therapist. She helped me work through the issues arising from my ill-fated marriage, but we'd barely touched on what she referred to as my old hometown and family issues. She sent me back to Oxley Crossing to confront the ghosts of my past. I'm doing that with a vengeance, alright."

A frown still creased Sean's brow. There was just so much he didn't know about this long-lost sister of his, and yet he couldn't help liking her.

"Your marriage?" he asked diffidently. "Was it really so bad?"

Blank-eyed, Kat looked through him. Remembering. Which immediately sobered her.

"I made a huge mistake. Trusted Bobby. Heart, body, soul. Right up till the time I didn't. When the shit hit the fan and I found out how badly he'd betrayed me, I went off the rails for a bit. Lost myself in the bottom of a bottle. Just like the Old Man. I'm more like him than is comfortable, Sean. Difference is, I saw where I was headed and pulled myself up before I lost everything I'd worked so bloody hard for."

She looked her shocked brother in the eye.

"I'm not an alco like Dad, but I came too close for comfort. I've sworn off alcohol. Total abstinence. The only foolproof cure."

Kat glanced sidelong at her brother.

"I went to Helga for help when I had trouble sleeping. She reckons I've still got a load of bad experiences to come to terms with, right back to before Mum died. So, there you have it, Sean."

Kat flung her arms wide, getting up from the table to escape to her room before her brother had her spilling any more of her dirty little secrets. Like the other dangerous behaviour for which she had also self-prescribed abstinence, though not necessarily total. Not all the time. She liked sex. Who didn't? But she made sure it was discreet, and *always* on her terms. A tantalising image of Charlie Reynolds flickered in the back of her mind.

6

"Hold the bus!"

Kat dived out of Sean's ute and raced across the service station apron to the bus idling by the side of the road. Half in, half out, the driver, more concerned with not spilling his take-away coffee than his passengers, looked back over his shoulder, and gave her a wave.

The disturbing conversation with her brother the night before had resulted in a sleepless night for Kat. It wasn't the first she'd experienced due to bad memories, so much more debilitating than a medical emergency, and she was sure it wouldn't be the last. Unfortunately, it did mean she woke behind schedule and missed breakfast in her mad scramble to catch the bus to Tamworth. Ten seconds later she slung her bag onto the vacant front seat, pulling out her wallet to pay for the ticket. An excruciatingly slow two hours later, she alighted in front of the Tamworth Railway Station. The terminus.

She yawned, then stepped out smartly to claim one of only two taxis in sight to take her across town to pick up the Honda Odyssey.

Even though it was ready to drive away, there were still so many warranty, registration, and insurance forms to fill in she was about ready to gnaw her arm off before she pulled in at the café across from the homewares superstore for her belated breakfast.

Make that brunch, she thought, practically inhaling her bacon and mushroom omelette and pot of good strong Aussie tea. A quick phone call to alert her arranged shopping guide, and she crossed the street, mentally bracing herself for the ordeal ahead.

Which turned out not quite the ordeal she'd feared, as Anthea, her guide, had prepared an even more detailed list than she had. With no dithering, and only an occasional hesitation to consider colour, fabric or style, Kat and Anthea swept through departments selling white goods, kitchen and dining to entertaining, lounge and bedroom suites in record time. No department was missed, and none required a second visit.

It still took Kat hours to fully equip her house down to the last teaspoon and dish towel, but with a quick break for lunch, they were finished mid-afternoon. Anthea, with her combination of super efficiency and great sense of humour had turned what Kat had expected to be an awful chore into an almost pleasurable experience. The delivery of flowers, champagne and chocolates Kat ordered as a thank-you gift for her were well-earned.

A few more purchases in more specialised shops and she hit the road for home. It set off what felt more like a flock of stampeding emus than butterflies in her stomach to realise Oxley Crossing was indeed home once again.

~~~~~
~~~~~

It was almost dark when Kat arrived back, and once again, bless his boots, Sean had the kids organised and a meal ready to serve. She really was going to miss him when he left in the morning.

"That was good, Sean." Kat eased back from the table. "It sure is a relief to finally be able to slow down. I feel I've been running at warp speed since Monday morning."

Her brother's good-natured snicker was predictable, and, without looking, Kat grinned and flashed him her middle finger.

"Seriously, though, Kat, have you got everything? I'll stay longer if you need me, otherwise Robert's expecting me back on duty tomorrow night."

"Nah. It's all good. You've been wonderful, Bro, and while there's probably heaps I've missed, I've nailed the basics. Which reminds me, kids." She looked from one child to the next around the table. "With everything that needed doing, I've hardly had a moment to get to know you guys. Or you me. We'll have to work on that, won't we? I've been a loner for most of my life, so I'm not sure how I'll fit in as part of your family, but I'll give it my best shot."

Through quietly observant eyes, Kat noticed her sister's worried frown deepening steadily.

"Something worrying you, Ailsa?"

With Kat's question, the girl flushed and hung her head.

"No. Not really. It's just … Kids at school today were talking, and I started wondering. Did you really want to be our guardian? No one else did. Not really." She cast a wary sidelong glance at Sean who had the grace to look abashed.

"You've been put to a lot of trouble. And expense. You don't even know us!"

"You've got me there, Ailsa," Kat admitted. "Actually, until Monday morning I didn't even know the five of you existed. But you know? It's like I told Sean yesterday. I chose to make the offer. I chose to become your guardian. My choice. Nobody forced me into it. I don't regret it for a moment, but I've been doing quite a bit of heavy thinking. I have no experience of family, or parenting, to fall back on, so I'm bound to make mistakes. You'll all have to help me out, I reckon."

She paused to see if there were any questions or comments, continuing slowly when her words were met by tense silence.

"I can't promise you'll be happy. Each and every one of us is responsible for our own happiness, you know. We can't rely on other people to *make* us happy. That comes from being true to ourselves. There are promises I will make, however. Promises I *will* keep."

She looked from one to the other again, finding them all focused intently upon her.

"As far as I'm humanly able, I'll keep you safe. That's what the 'guard' in guardian means. I'll keep a roof over your heads, food on the table and clothes on your backs. You'll be given every opportunity for an education to set you up to support yourselves as adults. I'll try to meet your *needs*, but some of your wants, like the fancy stuff your friends might have, I'll say no to."

"It sounds a lot more than we had before."

"Ailsa's right," Mickey agreed. "Only, ... What will you want from us in return?"

This question had them all looking anxious. They'd learnt early that helping hands often came with price tags.

What do I want?

It was a question Kat had asked herself often during recent months.

With a lop-sided grin, she answered their question and hers, relieving some of the tension. "I want a peaceful life." Kat's smile widened as she realised how very true that was. "Probably not going to get it, though," she added, her eyes settling on Dennis who squirmed under her gaze. "I'll settle for a reasonable level of co-operation."

"What about rules?" Dennis couldn't hold back any longer.

"Rules? The usual, I suppose," Kat shrugged. "No stealing, fighting, cheating, lying, etcetera. If you can't do it at school, you probably shouldn't do it at home. Ask permission, and when either Mrs Bardon or myself tells you to do something, do it. That's what I mean by co-operation. You don't need me to spell it all out in every last little detail, do you? Just think for yourselves and do what's right, for God's sake."

"Mrs Johnson's always telling us to think for ourselves." Estelle nodded to herself.

"She's our teacher," Clarice elucidated, adding, "Stell and me are always good. We don't like getting in trouble."

Kat had noticed their tendency to evade notice, and grinned, understanding precisely what they meant. "Then I reckon we'll get along just fine."

With their knack for self-effacement, she'd need to beware those two didn't slip under her radar.

No child was going to be neglected on her watch. Or abused. That was her promise to whatever power ruled the Universe.

"Yes," Ailsa agreed. "We're glad you've taken us all on, and we won't make trouble for you, Kat, but ..." A child reared in poverty, she reverted to her earlier concern. "We're costing you an awful lot. Are you sure you can afford us? Mrs Walsh, my friend Sonia's mum, she's always going on about how she can't afford things, and she's only got Sonia and her little brother to buy stuff for."

Kat had been expecting someone, and not necessarily one of the kids, to raise the issue of money. You couldn't go on the sort of spending spree she had this week without it being noticed. And commented on.

She drew in a breath and trotted out the stock answer she'd prepared, since she'd be damned if she let on to anyone the true state of her satisfactorily healthy finances. Then they'd be wanting to know where the money came from.

"It has been expensive, setting up a proper home for all of us, but it's within what I originally budgeted for my new life back in Australia. I owned my home, a condo in the best part of San Francisco, and got a good price when I sold it. Then the exchange rate worked in my favour, and so did the country real estate prices. There won't be as much left over to invest as if I'd been on my own, but you haven't bankrupted me, Ailsa. I'm really good at managing money, so I won't let it come to that. Another promise."

She looked round the table again, noting the younger children becoming restless.

"No more questions? Then how about a game?"

Mickey produced a dog-eared pack of cards and a noisy game of *Go Fish* filled in the time till bed.

~~~~~

Beethoven dragged Kat out of a sound sleep several hours later. It took a moment for her to collect her wits and answer the phone, hoping no-one else had been woken by it.

"Sorry to disturb you, Dr Murphy. Oxley Crossing Hospital here. We'd appreciate it if you could come in."

Monday was her official starting date, but there was no way Kat could refuse an emergency call. She dragged on jeans and a jumper and crept out.

A crepuscular glow was spreading across the top of the hills several hours later when she emerged from the hospital after filling in the patient records and taking a last peep at Oxley Crossing's newest and youngest resident.

A small red Mitsubishi pulled in beside her as she unlocked her car.

"Oh, good. I'm so glad I caught you before you left."

The next second, Eddie Patterson enveloped her in a warm, scented embrace.

"I just had to thank you for coming to the rescue last night when our Megan was in so much trouble. Jon says it's thanks to you, Kat, that my grandson was delivered safely, and his mother's doing well today."

Kat's tired brain took a moment to compute the Patterson family tree. She'd recognised her patient immediately, surprised at how little Megan had changed.
~~~~~

She and Megan Patterson – now Megan Armitage – had been at school together, Megan a year or two behind her. Until now she hadn't made the link to Eddie, whom she still thought of as Eddie Turner.

"Mike and I stayed with little Chloe last night, but when Jon rang to say Megan and Joel were both safe, I cut these and dashed round with them to say thank you."

She placed a huge bouquet of roses in Kat's arms.

"You're welcome, Eddie, but I wasn't alone. The nurses did a fantastic job, you know. You should be thanking them."

"Oh, I will be, only I was lucky enough to catch you first. I've got more roses for them, too. And there's no need for false modesty, Dr Murphy," Eddie spoke quite severely. "Jon told me if you hadn't been here there might have been a vastly different outcome. We're all so very grateful."

Eddie retrieved another huge bunch of fragrant blooms from the back of her car and headed for the front door. Kat drove off, changing her direction a minute later. Doubling back through town, she took the road out to the cemetery. On Monday she'd been taken by surprise, and hadn't had a minute to herself since.

~~~~~

"Hello Mum. This is one for the books, isn't it? Me back in The Crossing. Bet you thought you'd never see the day."

Perched on a crumbling corner of Monica Murphy's grave, Kat let her thoughts spill out. It felt good to talk to her mother again. Even though she knew nobody was listening, the image of her beloved mother filled her heart and mind.
~~~~~

The distinctive scent of wattle blooming close by mingled with the pervasive tang of eucalyptus to perfume the crisp air filling her lungs. Birds rustled in the bushes, calling morning greetings to one another. For the very first time since walking off the plane at Mascot, Kat felt she was truly home again. Home in Australia.

Sydney, with its bustling crowds and traffic jams had never been home, although, like every bushie in the Big Smoke, she did enjoy the beaches. On the drive north, she'd been too tied up in knots to relax and absorb the scenery. Since then, well, since then she'd been frantically controlling her incipient panic, concentrating on doing what needed doing. One fraught step at a time. This morning, finally, she had time to sit and smell the gum trees, and know she was home.

Kat smiled, chatting on. As close to carefree as she'd been in a long, long while.

"How about the pack of kids I've inherited, Mum? I reckon I'll be dropping by to ask your advice fairly often."

For some time the idea of adoption had been tucked away in the most remote back corner of her mind. For future consideration. Now she thought of it, maybe that was where her offer had sprung from, shocking the socks off her, along with everyone else.

"Five is a bit extreme, though," she confided, "but, really, Mum, what else could I do?"

Kat thought about the options. She could have said she'd take one. Or two. Leaving behind … Who? Mickey, valiantly shouldering responsibilities far too heavy for his slender shoulders?

Or maybe shy, nervous Ailsa, with her ever-watchful eyes. Ready to put herself between the younger kids and danger. And no way could she have left Dennis whose outspoken bumptiousness covered a deep-seated fragility which made her heart ache. Or the aloof, self-contained twins who appeared two sides of a double-headed penny, but whom she suspected each had their own distinctive personalities.

"What would you have done, Mum? I just bet you'd have opened up your arms and gathered them in. I don't know if I'm what *they* need, but you know, Mum, I've got a sneaking suspicion they may be exactly what *I* need."

She hoped to God that in her inexperience, she didn't mess those poor kids up worse than they already had been.

Colin Murphy had a lot to answer for.

And isn't he in the right place to do just that?

The wicked thought made her grin. She'd remember that when the results of his deeds drove her to curse him in future.

Changing the subject, she continued chatting with her mother.

"Looks like Bridget tidied up around you recently. I'm glad. I know how important clean and tidy is to you. What do you think of these roses, then? Eddie's finest. I'll just get rid of these flowers that are past their prime and refill your vases."

Getting up, Kat looked around for the nearest tap, chatting on while she went about her task.

"Eddie was right, you know, Mum."

She went over the event in her mind, reviewing her actions.

Satisfied she'd made the right decisions, she continued.

"Good as the local midwives are, that baby could have been in real trouble if I hadn't been there. For him and Megan. He'd got himself in a pickle and was in too much of a hurry to wait for the ambulance to ship Megan off to Tamworth. Typical boy, huh. Now I really understand why the whole town was so desperate for a doctor. I'd forgotten how time and distance mean the difference between life and death in the bush. Makes me feel good about taking on the practice. I'm really needed here. Well, I'll be off for some sleep, Mum, but I'll be a regular visitor from now on. Now I'm back."

She couldn't quite bring herself to call The Crossing home. Physically it was, but in her heart? No. Just ... No.

There were too many blooms for the small vases flanking Monica's headstone. Impulsively, Kat crossed to where a mound of bare earth covered in a scatter of wilted flowers marked Colin and Therese Murphy's resting place. It would be some time before the ground settled and the grave could be finished neatly.

"Hello Therese. We never did get to meet, but I thought you might like to know your children will be okay. I'll take good care of them. I always wanted kids of my own, you know, so they'll be filling a gap in my life. I'll pop in from time to time and keep you posted."

She carefully lay a perfect yellow rose on top of the mound. Then, after a moment's consideration, a white one beside it.

"As for you, you good-for-nothing old reprobate, you better be on your best behaviour if you want St Peter to open up to you. You really pissed me off big-time, getting yourself killed before I could tell you what I thought of you," she berated.

"I had hoped you might have cleaned up your act, but that was too much to hope for, wasn't it?"

Against the odds, she'd made a success of her life, in spite of him. She stood up, her sudden burst of anger dissipating as she took in the beauty of the morning mist eddying low to the ground under the gum trees.

Morning mist, she thought, recalling a half-remembered poem she'd read once, her mood turning philosophical. *Veils of mist. Mourning veils. Well, we are in a cemetery.*

Not one for pretty words, it was as close as she came to poetry. Far more fitting, she felt, was the celebration hymn, sung by a butcher bird, the mastersinger of the Australian bush, which soared to the Heavens, praising God and his Faithful who lay in His holy ground. Kat's heart soared in harmony.

The man watching her felt his stomach lurch. Kat Murphy looked so damn good, smiling to herself and striding out as if she owned the world. Seeing her made him want things he knew he had no right wanting. And wanted, all the same.

A tingle between her shoulder blades slowed Kat's exit from the cemetery. She wasn't alone. Someone was watching her. Sensing no threat, she casually stepped aside from her path, halting in front of Michael the Archangel, standing tall and proud over the grave of Tobias Morgan, The Crossing's founding father. Surreptitiously, she scanned the trees which made the cemetery such a private place. There. Warmth suffused her body on recognising Charlie Reynold's tall, broad-shouldered figure half-hidden behind a massive Sandra Gordon grevillea weighed down with pale creamy-yellow spider flowers. Time for more aversion therapy?

Her cheerful grin widened, becoming distinctly wicked.

"Planning on revamping The Crossing's Dead Centre, Charlie?"

Damn! Charlie swore under his breath. The woman had eyes in the back of her head. He'd deliberately kept still, hoping to go unseen and avoid her altogether. It was bad enough he'd agreed to plant her trees for her. He was not – definitely was not – going to get involved with her. She'd turn his life upside down, and for what? Nothing, that's what. As soon as she discovered the truth, she'd drop him. Just like Renee had. Unfortunately, avoidance was out of the question this morning. What the hell was she doing here at this hour, anyway?

"Morning, Kathleen. Been saying your goodbyes?"

"Hellos more like. My Mum." She waved a careless hand in the direction Monica lay. "You?"

Charlie shrugged. "Grandad. I often drop in when I'm out jogging early. Keep his plot tidy. How come you're out and about at this hour?" If she was going to make a habit of these early morning visits he'd have to keep a wary eye out so as not to run into her again.

"Hospital called me last night. A bit of happy gossip. You won't beat Eddie, but you won't be far behind. Megan Armitage had a baby boy last night. Joel. My first patients. I'm so glad it's a story with a happy ending for my first." Abruptly the smile left her face.

"I owe you an apology, Charlie."

"Huh? An apology for what?" She didn't know she tied his gut in knots, did she?

"Demanding you give my commission priority, as if you had nothing else to do. I had a bright idea and acted on it without thinking. You should have told me to wait my turn."

"Might have to yet. Not sure I can get those fancy end-posts you want by the weekend."

Challenging Fate, Kat leaned closer, slipping her arm through his and smiling up at him again as they wended their way through the maze of headstones towards the carpark where her bright yellow RAV4 reflected back the rising sun. A sudden hunger for something other than food nearly made her let go. His tiny shudder telling her he was as aware of her as she was of him had her contrarily tightening her grip.

"Hang on! Back up Charlie."

No longer teasing, Kat clung to him, needing his support. She stared down at the headstone she'd glimpsed out of the corner of her eye.

Conrad Stephen Grant

&

Richard John Grant

Dearly beloved sons of Henry and Wilma Grant.

Together in death as in life.

R.I.P.

Con and Rick?

Dead?

Kat's legs turned to jelly, her breath hitching in her chest. Her arms came up in goosebumps. Although mentally braced to meet the Grant twins in the street, this encounter was so unexpected it threw her off-balance. She read the inscription again, noting the single date at the bottom. They'd died on the same day, three years after she left Oxley Crossing. So long ago. Recovering quickly, sudden anger burned in her gut. Whatever tragedy had befallen the Grants, it had been well-deserved.

The beauty of the morning no longer charmed her.

"Gotta go. I'm starving. Call me if you have to cancel our working bee this weekend, Charlie." She dropped his arm and began walking, speaking to him over her shoulder.

"Er ... Yeah. Sure."

"See you then, Charlie Reynolds."

What in hell got into her? Charlie pushed back his battered Akubra, watching Kat's hasty retreat.

Something to do with the Grants? Nothing came to mind. They were before his time. He read the brief inscription, gaining no insight there, but he was sure it was seeing their grave that had set her off. Something niggled in the back of his mind. Some passing remark he'd half-heard yesterday down at Tan's.

Kat's pace picked up as she approached her car. Safely inside, she took a moment to bring her chaotic emotions under control before driving off, wheels spinning in the gravel.

Who'd have bloody believed it!

The Grant boys. Dead.

Parking next to Sean's ute minutes later, a question popped into her mind.

If I'd known they were dead, would I have come home sooner?

7

Shading her eyes from the sun, Kat watched Sean's ute dwindle into the heat haze rising from the bitumen, remembering the last time she'd said goodbye to him. Today she knew where he was headed. Knew she'd see him again. Then, he'd woken her at dawn, told her he had a job as roustabout with the shearers who'd been working out at the Lanner's place, and snuck out and away before she was properly awake. Before their father could stop him. She'd missed him. She missed him again. Already.

She wiped her eyes, telling herself it was tiredness and the bright sunshine making her eyes water. Nothing the nap she'd promised herself wouldn't cure.

Waking, refreshed, a couple of hours later, she lay for a while, thinking. About the Grant twins, Con and Ricky. Wondering if the rest of the family still lived out at *Willowglen*. Were they the source of the resurrected stories both Fran Porteous and Fiona MacIntosh had mentioned? Kat had no trouble believing the Grants could hold a grudge that long. Deliberately, she put them out of her mind.

If she had to deal with the Grants down the track, then would be soon enough. No point in borrowing trouble. This was Oxley Crossing.

If Trouble was looking for Kat Murphy, it would find her soon enough.

Recalling the birth of baby Joel Armitage brought her smile back. Crawling out of bed, she showered and dressed, scooped up her keys, and headed into town to pay a visit to her first, and, so far, only patients. In the rear-view mirror she saw the boxes and baskets Sean had helped her pack before he left. She'd go to the hospital first, then haul this stuff the kids wanted to keep into the house. It was pitifully little, spread between five. She'd brought more with her from the States than this. Which reminded her, she needed to give her new address to the shipping company.

An unexpected treasure discovered during the packing and clearing out had been her mother's photo albums. Along with the few pieces of Monica's wedding china which had survived, they had been safe inside the bottom of her china cabinet which Sean and Mickey had loaded into his ute and brought up yesterday afternoon. They held too many precious memories of her mother to be thrown out with the rubbish.

"Hello Megan. You're looking perkier." Kat breezed into her patient's room. "And how's young Joel? I can't wait to get my hands on him again. I do love babies."

She winked at Megan and crossed over to gently lift the sleeping baby from his father's arms. Cuddling him, she read his chart, and his mother's, then shooed Jon out while she examined mother and baby, pronouncing them both thriving.

"He's strong, Megan, and so are you. Remember, tell the nurses if you're worried about anything. They seem to be a really experienced team, and I'm only five minutes away if I'm needed."

Leaving Megan, she was side-tracked by Fran Porteus who wanted her to take a look at one of the aged-care residents who'd fallen in the shower that morning, so it was some time before she made her way back to her car.

Detouring down the main street a while later, she stopped in at the supermarket, then the butcher. Five kids to be fed meant she had to cook tonight. Pity Sean had had to leave. A woman could get used to coming home to an appetising meal on the table.

"Hello," she said, breezing up to the counter. Then she took a second look at the woman serving her. "It is you, isn't it? Marcia Jensen? You barely look a day older, Marcia."

"Kind of you to say so, Kathleen, only it's not Jensen any longer."

Kat noted Marcia's use of her name lacked the intimate warmth Charlie's had carried. The hackles on the back of her neck bristled, although she kept her expression carefully neutral.

Marcia lifted her chin a defiant notch.

"My name's Whitman, now. I married Tony. We've got two sons, Jeremy and Luke."

"Good for you, Marcia. Tony always was sweet on you." Another connection clicked in her mind. "Your Luke. He and Dennis are friends, aren't they?"

"That's right," Marcia nodded.

Kat groaned mentally. Damn connections. However, putting her little brother's interests before her own, she answered pleasantly. And, surprising herself, sincerely.

"He was telling me how you give him hugs, same as you do Luke. I think he secretly wishes you were his mum. I'm so glad you were there for him, Marcia. I look forward to meeting your Luke once we're settled."

She bought mince for the pasta she planned for dinner, then turned to go. "See you around, Marcia."

It had been a bit of a strain, being pleasant in the face of Marcia's coolness.

"Wait!"

Kat let her hand slip from the door handle, looking back to see Marcia scurrying round the end of the counter.

"Kathleen … Kat … I'm sorry." She offered her hand. "I know we weren't ever friends, but school was a long time ago. Do you think we could start again? As adults? It's just … I was always so jealous of you."

Startled, Kat stared at her.

"Jealous? Of me?" She laughed. "Got that the wrong way round, haven't you, Marcia? You were the popular girl who had everything. *I* envied *you*."

Marcia blushed. "I used to think it was you Tony was interested in."

Kat's mouth dropped open.

"He was forever talking to you on the veranda between lessons. I could see from my classroom across the quad."

"You goose!" A ripple of laughter escaped Kat. "I used to help him with his homework. So he could impress *you* with how smart he was. It was worth it to have him stand up for me against the bullies."

Another forgotten friendship? Kat relaxed, more at ease now.

"Oh." Marcia's pale cheeks flared again.

"You know, I like the idea of starting fresh with you, Marcia. I don't have too many friends in this town. Could sure use one more."

"I reckon you'll have more now than you used to, now you're flavour of the month."

If there was still a green tinge to Marcia's comment, Kat chose to ignore it.

"Speaking of the old days, you don't happen to know what's become of the Grants, do you?"

In spite of Kat's deliberate nonchalance, that question earned her a hard stare. Where Kat Murphy was concerned, the Grants had been the opposite of friends, a fact Marcia well remembered.

"Them!" She curled her lip, dropping her animosity to become sisters-in-arms. "They tried it on with me too, you know, but Tony told them where they could stick their parties down by the creek. Both boys died, you know. Smashed themselves up driving home stoned out of their minds. Not long after, the family sold up and moved interstate. Dad said the cop who took over when Trelawney was transferred made life too hot for them. That was the man before Don Matthews who's here now."

How fortuitous.

Relieved, Kat was glad Marcia had buried her old animosity. If enough people wished her well, she might even develop something resembling a social life.

"I've got to get a move on, Marcia, but why don't we get together for lunch one day soon?"

"Sounds good, Kat. See you then." This time Marcia's smile was genuine.

~~~~~

Friday. Moving day. Anthea had called her late the afternoon before. "The truck's loaded, Kat," she'd assured her, "ready to move out first thing. I've double checked the inventory, and they'll be in Oxley Crossing by nine."

At eight-thirty Kat was on site. She opened the doors and windows to air the house, and sat waiting on the front step, cup of tea in hand. Fortunately, the driver was as good as his word. She'd barely taken her first sip when the carrier Anthea had booked pulled up out front. Five minutes later Sam and Russell Gill arrived. From then on it was full steam ahead until every piece of furniture was in its right place and every rug unrolled and in position, deadening the empty-house echoes.

Carriers and handymen, their work finished, had all left, and Kat was alone in the kitchen unpacking and washing china and glassware when the children arrived home from school, a whirlwind of excitement bursting through the door.

"Oh, wow," Dennis exclaimed in round-eyed awe.

"This is so cool. Just wait till Luke sees that humongous tele. It's way bigger than his."
~~~~~

Similar sentiments were echoed in differing words by the other children as they darted from room to room, exploring.

"Right," Kat called them to order. "There's juice, and the last of Sean's cookies. Take it out to the barbecue deck. Then I've got jobs for all of you before you disappear."

"Jobs?"

"Yes, little brother. Jobs." Kat's grin showed almost as many teeth as a crocodile's. "You didn't expect me to unpack your personal stuff, did you? Or make your beds up? Then there's the rest of the linen and kitchen gadgets to sort. I need help."

None of them had given the necessary chores a thought.

"Right. C'mon you lot. Give a hand." Mickey, recalling his sister's wish for co-operation, chivvied the younger ones. "Where do we start, Kat?"

The house finally organised to Kat's satisfaction, she sent them off to shower and change, heading to her own room to do likewise.

"How come you want us to have our baths so early?"

"Oh, didn't I mention? I haven't had time to shop or cook today, so we're having dinner down the pub. Where we all went for lunch on Monday."

"Terrific. Mrs Morris is the best cook in town. At least that's what my friend Molly Tan says." Estelle clapped her hands, blushing when she caught Kat's raised eyebrow. Not that Kat considered herself in the running for such a prestigious title.

"Molly might even be there." Clarice turned excitedly to Kat. "Her family are always going there for dinner on Friday night."

"I hope they're there tonight. Won't she be surprised to see us." They ran off to put on the flower-girl dresses they'd worn when their other friend, Gwynna's mum had married Joey Lambert not long before.

Listening to the excited chatter, Kat concluded eating out was an exceptionally rare treat. One she decided would be less rare in future.

The dining room at *The Victoria Inn* had never been this well patronised in the past, Kat observed, nodding to a few familiar faces. It seemed every man and his dog was there.

"Lots of people like to come on Friday nights," Mickey explained, leaning close to be heard above the hum of multiple conversations.

Just then the door from the main bar opened to admit another party of diners.

"I see that Murphy slut's here. Ought to be ashamed of herself, lording it over us. Doctor! Hah! You won't catch me taking my kids to *her*. Can't imagine she's changed, no matter what Bill Whitman says."

The strident female tones filled a momentary silence. A silence which deepened as shocked faces turned from the speaker to the table where Kat and the children sat.

"That does it! You shut your nasty mouth, Janet Simmonds!"

Attention abruptly swung to centre on quiet, placid Dorothy James who'd sprung to her feet, her chair screeching against the polished floorboards with the force of her movement. A hectic flush staining her cheeks, Dot's eyes were riveted on the woman who had spoken so disparagingly of Kat Murphy.

"I never did understand how any so-called intelligent person could believe what those bullying Grants and their toadies said. Liars, thieves and bullies those boys were. I'll have you know, Janet Simmonds, Kathleen Murphy was a decent, hard-working girl who never mixed with their wild crowd. And she wasn't mixed up with Fred Hayes's nefarious goings-on in here, either, in spite of what *some* people said. I could see what went on over here from my cottage next door, and I'm telling you, when Kathleen finished work in the kitchen, she went straight home with her father."

"Oh, yeah? So how come you never said anything at the time?"

While all eyes were focused on Dot and Janet, Kat quietly got to her feet and went to stand beside Dot James whose stricken expression tore at her heart.

"Because, Janet Simmonds," Kat stated dryly, "as you know very well, your husband being his best mate, Alf would have thumped the living daylights out of Dot if she'd drawn attention to herself by speaking out about something he considered to be none of her business. Those cottage windows had a two-way view. I knew what was going on, but I was just a kid. Nobody listened to *me*. I didn't see you coming to Dot's assistance, did I, Janet? It wasn't only the school which suffered from a culture of systemic bullying."

"Ladies."

Phil Morris bustled through from the bar to pour oil on the troubled waters. Or maybe some other form of libation, Kat thought, cynically noting the barmaids following him laden with bottles they quietly used to top up glasses around the room.

"Ladies," Phil rumbled. "All those old stories reflect badly on our town and are surely best forgotten. The Oxley Crossing I know is a very different place to when Fred Hayes ruled the roost. As Dr Murphy said, she was just a kid. She's done really well for herself, growing up to become a doctor. We're lucky to have her. I say, we ought to make her welcome. Raise your glasses in a toast to our new doc. Dr Kathleen Murphy."

The resulting whispers stilled, silence reigning again when Poppy MacIntosh rose stiffly to her feet, imperiously tapping on her glass for attention.

"Mum, sit down." Fiona tugged vainly at her mother's skirt, her hand impatiently swatted away.

"I've got something long overdue to say, and I'm going to say it," Poppy hissed back, arthritic hands gripping the back of her chair as if her life depended on not letting go. She gazed slowly round the room, gathering her thoughts.

"You all know me," she began. "I taught a lot of you, or your children. I came to Oxley Crossing when Kathleen Murphy was in her last year of school. The stories I heard about her horrified me. All the more as I got to know her and realised how completely false they were. When I spoke up, I was told I was too new to know anything, but I had eyes, and ears. I knew the difference between those vicious fabrications and the truth."

She looked certain people in the eye, issuing a silent challenge, then continued.

"I saw other things too. Besides what went on here in the pub, there was corruption at Council level. When I complained, I was told I had no proof. That if I knew what was good for me, I'd keep my mouth shut.

She patted Fiona's hand.

"Those threats were reinforced by acts of vandalism against my home. When my daughter, Fiona was threatened, I did shut up. I'm sorry now that I took the coward's way out."

This time her challenging stare was grim. Tight-lipped.

"Never forgot, though. A year or two later the town began to change. Sergeant Trelawney left under a cloud. Bill Whitman and his friends ousted the corrupt element in the Shire Council. Fred Hayes sold the hotel, and the town flourished under new, honest leadership until it became what it is today. But I believe Phil is wrong in saying we should forget the evils of the past. Put them behind us, certainly. Forget them, no, or we'll be doomed to suffer them again one day. I say we should be vigilant, and root out evil whenever it raises its head. Before it can take hold. I offer you another toast."

Poppy raised her glass high, her voice carrying to all corners of the room.

"To a future which is happy and peaceful because we are strong enough, and smart enough, to learn from the mistakes of the past, and not repeat them."

"Well said, Poppy." Barbara Morgan rose to her feet at the next table. "Let's make sure Oxley Crossing continues to be a town worth living in. It's up to us."

After that it seemed anticlimactic to simply continue eating dinner as if nothing had happened.

"Kat, what was all that about?" Mickey leaned close so his voice didn't carry to other tables. The younger children listened hard.

"Like those two courageous women, Dot and Poppy, said," Kat replied, her tone deliberately normal. She didn't care who overheard her. "The Crossing used to be a very different place. Fortunately, it's changed for the better."

"But, what did they mean about stories about you, Kat? Why did that woman call you a slut?"

"Oh, Ailsa. I refused to kow-tow to the bullies, so they got even by making up dreadful stories. None of them were true."

"Like internet trolls?"

"Exactly like trolls."

"That's mean."

"It was, and they were. All you need to know about those stories is, I never did anything for which I need to be ashamed. I can hold my head up, and so can all of you."

8

"We're not staying for dessert, kids. Not tonight. Let's go for ice-creams at the garage, instead."

Sticking to her edict over a chorus of grumbled protests, Kat made sure she left the dining room as quickly as she could. She'd had enough of past evils for one night. Getting caught up in rehashing ancient history was so not her scene.

She made it outside, but there her luck ran out.

"Evening Kathleen. Kids."

"Hi Charlie."

"Did you know we moved into our new house today, Mr Reynolds?"

"Sure did, Clarice. Must be really exciting for you."

Kat stood aside while the children crowded around Charlie, eagerly regaling him with descriptions of their new home.

"Kids, do you mind if I have a word with Kathleen?" It being clear he meant a private word, they politely moved away.

Almost out of earshot.

"Are you okay, Kathleen?"

Charlie reached for her hand, ignoring the tingles arising from the contact. Just as he ignored the extra warmth flooding his body. What he'd heard in the hotel tonight had clarified the whispers he'd overheard yesterday, rousing him to anger on Kat's behalf.

Already unsettled by the confrontation with Janet Simmonds and the buzz of whispers which had followed, Kat was tempted to lean into the warmth flowing from their joined hands. To accept comfort.

A temptation she resisted.

Accepting comfort led to dangers of the heart she preferred not to risk. Not here, and not now. Withdrawing her hand, she stepped back. The icy crackle in her voice reflected the chill she felt on losing Charlie's warmth.

"Perfectly okay. Why wouldn't I be, Charlie?"

He winced mentally, knowing he'd overstepped.

However, now he'd opened his mouth he was damned if he'd back down. He wished he'd done what he really wanted and simply waded in, wrapped both arms around her and hugged her.

For some reason he chose not to question, Kathleen Murphy mattered. To him. Personally. Too much.

Maybe he should simply give in and see where this mad attraction took him, instead of fighting against it.

"I was in the bar," he explained, ploughing doggedly on.

"With the door wide open, everyone heard what Janet Simmonds said. And what came after. Decent of Dot and Poppy to defend you. It was all before my time, but it didn't take a genius to realise you'd been badly maligned back when you were just a kid. I hope to God it's not going to make things difficult for you now, in your practice."

He couldn't help wondering if there were others like Janet Simmonds who weren't happy with the new doctor.

"Their choice, Charlie. Guess I'll find out Monday. Either patients will turn up, or they won't. Either way, I'll be there for those who need me."

Ignoring him when he followed, she strode over to join the children who were waiting beside the car, agog with poorly disguised curiosity.

"We're going for ice-cream, Charlie. Why don't you join us?" Ailsa, showing an early propensity for the matchmaking which had become a favourite pastime of The Crossing's womenfolk, invited, casting a wary, sly glance in Kat's direction.

"Sure. Why not?" Against the warnings of his inner voice, Charlie jumped at the unlooked-for opportunity to spend more time with Kat, and, maybe, make up the ground he'd lost. With a conspiratorial smile for Ailsa, he ignored Kat's exasperated huff.

"Where's your truck?" Mickey was looking round the carpark.

"Walked in."

"Then we'll give you a lift," Mickey offered, looking away when Kat rolled her eyes.

So much for keeping my distance from Charlie Reynolds.

If only she could go back to thinking of being in his proximity as aversion therapy. Unfortunately, with her physical response to him strengthening with each encounter rather than waning, she was pretty sure that wasn't going to work.

*Why stress? Enjoy while you can. Nothing will come of it anyway. Whatever **it** is.*

She wished her inner woman would stop whispering wicked temptations.

~~~~~

"Hello Aunt Eddie! Hello Mr Patterson!"

Ailsa smiled at the couple who had been long-term benefactors of herself and her siblings.

"Why, hello to you too, Ailsa dear. All of you. And you as well, Charlie Reynolds." This last was uttered in Eddie Patterson's driest tone, and with a questioning lift of her brow. She'd done her darnedest to draw Charlie into the fold and pair him up with one of The Crossing's single women, finally admitting a rare defeat. Now here he was trotting in at Kat Murphy's heels. A frown creased his forehead as usual, but still … Eddie narrowed her eyes. He looked indefinably different. She'd be keeping a close eye on that pair. Out of sight under the table she crossed her fingers, sending up a silent prayer that something good would come of this budding friendship.

"We're here for ice-cream," Estelle announced, skipping across to the freezer to choose her favourite.

"Water for me," Kat murmured when Charlie waved her to follow the kids.
~~~~~

Mike rose to his feet to take care of the influx of customers.

"Make mine a coffee, Mike." Charlie handed over his card.

"Why don't you two sit here with Mike and I while the kids enjoy their treat."

Eddie patted a vacant place at her table. She already had the conversation mapped out in her mind. Innocuous talk about the baby, then she'd move on to more serious topics.

"Did you know Megan and baby Joel came home from hospital this afternoon? He's such a good baby, isn't he Mike?" Eddie turned to her husband for corroboration, rattling on without letting him get a word in edgewise.

Grinning, he waited till their guests were safely corralled for Eddie's delicate interrogation, then slid a coffee in front of Charlie and reclaimed his chair. Just minutes earlier his wife had received a startling call from her bosom-bow, Hazel Whitman, a Friday night regular at the pub. To think there'd been such stirring goings-on, and Eddie not present! Mike knew she was itching to investigate the matter further, and here came Kat Murphy, one of the principals, sauntering through the door. The perfect person to satisfy her curiosity.

If Kat was in the mood to play along.

"Hear things got a bit lively down the pub tonight?" Mike figured it was part of his husbandly duty to start the ball rolling. Besides, he freely admitted to considerable curiosity of his own.

Only Kat resisted the urge to spill her guts.

From the ensuing silence Mike thought for a bit he was going to be ignored, but finally Charlie put down his mug, and, casting an uncomfortable sidelong glance at Kat, muttered an answer.

"That old bat, Janet Simmonds was shooting her mouth off over past grievances, trying to upset Kat. Dot James set her straight."

"Janet's had a lot to bear, one way or another," Eddie said, "but still, that's no excuse for her sourness. Take no notice of her Kat, dear. I can assure you, the rest of us are overwhelmingly grateful you decided to give The Crossing a chance. I feel so guilty for not doing more to put a stop to that dreadful gossip back when you were a kid."

"You're being a bit hard on yourself, Eddie," Kat replied, surprising herself. "As I recall, you had your hands full with your husband in and out of chemo." Refusing to be drawn further, she shrugged and, lips quirking into a half-smile tacitly acknowledging Eddie's frustration, changed the subject.

"Actually, Mike," she said, turning her limpid gaze on him, "I'm glad of the opportunity to thank you for casting your vote in my favour the other night."

Mike chuckled. "Me and the rest of the committee. It was unanimous, you know. Fran Porteus was the one who best appreciated your qualifications, and when she waltzed in, waving your CV in the air and telling us we'd be fools to let you get away, we merely went through the motions. On the whole, I think everyone liked that you were a local girl come home. That rubbish Janet was spouting tonight was water under the bridge. All wrong then. Irrelevant now."

"Hopefully." Kat shrugged again, glancing pointedly at Charlie's empty cup. "If you're finished Charlie, I'd like to get these kids home."

Goodnights quickly exchanged, she hustled her family out the door. Seconds later they were all buckled up and ready to roll.

"You know, Kat? It's so good you're looking after us now," Dennis piped up from his place between the twins down the back. "I hate Mum and Dad. I'm glad they're dead."

"Dennis!"

Ailsa's hissed admonition was the only sound in a suddenly fraught silence.

Bloody Hell! It's one thing after another!

For a moment Kat almost wished she'd never come home, rather than have to face yet another difficult confrontation at the end of what had already been a very long day. With an audible sigh, she switched off the ignition and turned as far round as her seat allowed to face the kids.

"I'm glad to be looking after you too, Dennis. But the thing is, kids," her eyes moved slowly from one to the next, connecting intimately with all five, "hate is an awfully destructive emotion. When it's got nowhere to go, like when the person you hate is dead, it rebounds on you. It eats away at you from the inside, ending up making you feel bad about yourself. Maybe not straight away, but it's always there, waiting to hurt you. It's better to look for good, rather than dwell on the bad."

"You mean like ... we should forgive them for neglecting us? They were the ones at fault." Tersely belligerent, Mickey sided with his brother.

"Forgiveness is the ideal. It's healing, but it's very hard to achieve. Especially when you don't have all the facts." Kat debated with herself, then decided to tell them what she knew.

"I never knew your Mum," she began, "but Colin Murphy was my dad too, and my opinion of him was never very high. When my mother was alive, she kept him pretty much in line, but he was a weak man. A heavy drinker and a gambler. Which meant there was never enough money for the essentials, let alone extras. After she died, he went off the rails, becoming a weekend binge drinker. If we kids got in his way we'd cop a backhander pretty damn quick. Or worse."

Kat thought for a moment, feeling her way. "I was curious about him and your mother, so I looked up their medical records. Doc Roberts made copious notes on all his patients. You know, your mum made the old man quit his boozing before she married him. She was good for him and they seem to have been okay for the first few years."

"I ... I guess they were. I sorta remember. Mum used to laugh a lot. Do you remember, Ailsa?" Mickey looked at his sister, who nodded, although clearly not entirely sure she did.

"So what went wrong?" Mickey asked.

"Why did everything get so bad?"

"As far as I can tell from Doc Roberts's notes, the downhill slide started when your mum was expecting Dennis. She was a bit old to be having babies, and there were problems. After he was born, she was sick for a while, and never fully recovered. She found it hard going, and your father wasn't much help. He'd always reckoned children and household chores were women's work. Then your mum got pregnant with the twins before she was well enough to cope. Have you heard of post-natal depression?"

The children all looked blankly back at her, so Kat explained as simply as possible.

"Some women have a hard time after having a baby. Depression is like a black fog sucking all your energy out of you. Like that thing in Harry Potter. You can't think. You can't help yourself. It's a horrible, debilitating condition. Your father was away at work all day leaving your mum with no-one to help her. She simply couldn't cope with a houseful of babies. And your father couldn't cope either. He turned back to the drink, making the whole situation worse. After a while people noticed and Doc Roberts got involved, but by then your dad had become an alcoholic. Another debilitating condition. Neither of them was in any fit state to take care of kids."

Ailsa sniffed. "Sometimes we were so hungry I stole food from the shops." Mickey reached over and squeezed her hand.

"Your mum was slowly getting better, but she still had bad times. She got hold of illegal drugs from somewhere. When she took them she felt good for a while, even though they were really bad for her, so she kept taking them. Doc Roberts was trying to help her. Then the accident happened. And here we are."

"Mum was getting better," Ailsa commented. "She was starting to take better care of us all towards the end."

"Pity Dad didn't get better too. I feel sorry for us, not him." Dennis, still recalcitrant, chipped in from the back seat.

"I'm not making excuses for your parents, Dennis, only, you know? Ineffective parents though they were, they weren't evil or anything. However, I agree, you kids had much the worst of it, that's for damned sure. I just want you to understand the causes. For your own sakes."

Kat waited a moment, but it seemed no-one had more to say, so she closed the discussion.

"We'll leave it for now, but I'm here if any of you have questions at any time. Or if you just want to talk."

Kat waited a moment to see if anyone had any more to say. Silence reigned, so she restarted the engine and slipped the car into gear. She had a feeling this subject wasn't done with, not by a long shot, but she'd wait till one of the children brought it up again after they'd had time to think it through. It would be counter-productive to force the issue before they were ready.

Noticing Charlie who'd sat quietly, keeping out of the discussion, she smiled apologetically.

"Bet you wished you'd walked home after all," she murmured.

"Not at all," he murmured back. "I thought you handled that really well, Kathleen."

Listening, he'd discovered he had a very healthy respect for the enormity of the task Kat Murphy had taken on. These kids weren't going to be easy.

As if five kids would ever be easy!

~~~~~

Later that night, after the children were all asleep, tucked up in their new beds, in their new home, Kat's chamomile tea grew cold while her thoughts wandered.

Her mind filled with the information she'd shared with her young sibs, she found herself comparing her father's and Therese's plight with her own brush with depression and alcohol.
~~~~~

It wasn't so different, really, except that she had had no-one else dependent on her. Part of her problem, actually. Being alone. Well, she wasn't alone now, and these kids had been through enough to last anyone a lifetime. She'd be sure to keep her guard up and not backslide.

Half asleep on her comfortable new sofa, she realised what she'd told the kids was true. Though still awfully hard, forgiveness was easier when one had all the data.

Maybe I've forgiven the Old Bastard at last, she marvelled. *Now I just need to forgive myself.*

9

"Sit! Eat!"

"But Kat …," Mickey protested, pushing his chair back from the table. "Charlie just pulled in. He'll expect me to help him unload."

He most likely would, Kat silently agreed, recalling Charlie's instructions from the night before. When they'd dropped him off outside the nursery, he had told her he'd managed to acquire all the materials for her espaliered orchard and intended making an early start. Mickey was instructed to be ready to help, as was his mate, Jase Gibson, another of Charlie's young part-time workers. If they all got stuck into it, the job would be finished the same day.

Seven o'clock was a bit earlier than Kat had expected though, and she'd only just put breakfast on the table. She saw no reason for letting the bacon and eggs Mickey had asked for go to waste. A boy planning on a day of hard physical labour needed nourishment. Exasperated, Kat leaned a hand on his shoulder, holding him in place, repeating her admonition.

"Eat your breakfast, kid, just do it fast. I'll go chat Charlie up till you finish."

A bubble of quickly suppressed laughter rose in her chest as she strolled outside, swallowing a last healthy bite of the toast she'd scooped up from her own plate on the way out.

Kat's eyes flicked appreciatively over Charlie's tall, broad-shouldered body. Last night's half-hearted idea to go with the flow and give up fighting the hitch in her breath and the acceleration of her pulse every time she found herself in his wholly masculine presence, had become, overnight, a firm decision. It felt kind of liberating to admit to herself she found Charlie Reynolds sexy as hell. Silently she recalled the words she'd spoken to Mickey, laughter rising again. Maybe she ought to 'chat him up' and see where it got her.

"Morning Charlie. Can I interest you in a spot of breakfast? Coffee?"

"Nah, I'm fine."

"You sure are, Charlie Reynolds."

Kat's warm purr implied more than her words said. She deepened her smile, then, ignoring his startled, wary glance, she sashayed over to stand next to him, ostensibly checking out the load of fruit trees, logs, rolls of wire and bags of concrete on the back of the truck. Deliberately leaning close, her shoulder grazing his, she was shocked by the tingle shooting straight from that point of contact to the core of her womanhood.

Well. That was unexpected!

It took considerable effort to suppress any overt reaction.

To make it seem entirely natural when she moved away to lean over the tailgate inspecting the load.

"You reckon you can fit all that lot in alongside my driveway? Aren't you going to leave spaces between the trees?"

Charlie edged away, a red tinge creeping up his neck. For a moment he was so confused by the promise in her frank 'come on' he almost missed her utterly prosaic comment. He was damned if he knew where he stood with Kathleen Murphy. Just when he got used to her keeping her distance, here she was purring like a kitten inviting him to stroke. Hands tingling with the desire to do just that, he choked on the image which sprang into his mind.

She really was well-named, he thought, shoving his hands into the safety of his pockets. There was a distinct feline quality to Kathleen Murphy he hadn't noticed during their earlier encounters. He snuck a surreptitious glance, sheer lust threatening to overtake better judgement as he absorbed the back view of tiny denim cut-offs barely coving her nicely rounded derriere. He'd already copped an eyeful of long, lithe, bare legs as she'd emerged from the back door.

Fruit trees. She's talking about fruit trees. Charlie wrenched his mind back from the salacious depths into which it had sunk. He was here to work, not try it on with the new doc.

"Some are for the backyard, too, remember?" he muttered.

Kat laughed, and patted his arm.

"Of course. But, strewth, Charlie, that's a lot of trees. I was thinking orchard. Looks more like a damned forest."

"You said as many different varieties as I could fit. Have you gone and changed your mind? I didn't have you pegged as one of those women who never know what they want."

"Oh, I know what I want, Charlie." She turned to him, flicking an upward glance from beneath lowered lids.

Charlie's blood turned to molten lava. He moved round to the back of the truck to hide his body's treacherous response.

"I know what I want, and I'm positive you can deliver, Charlie," Kat reiterated with a bold, smiling glance which tacitly informed him the double entendre was deliberate.

A grunt was all the response he was capable of. Deliver? What exactly did the damned woman mean with her insinuations? Did she mean anything? Or was she just leading him on for the hell of it? Charlie sucked in a breath, feeling he'd just taken a sucker punch to the gut. Off and on all week stray thoughts of what he'd like to do with Kat Murphy if he got the chance had been drifting through his mind. Now it looked as if that chance might be forthcoming, he wasn't entirely sure he wanted to pursue it. He was afraid a woman of Kathleen Murphy's calibre would want more than he had to give. Fighting against his treacherous instincts Charlie reminded himself of the reason he'd elected to swear off women.

He couldn't give Kat Murphy what she wanted, so any relationship with her was doomed to failure from the start.

Better not to start. He didn't do relationships.

He was relieved beyond measure to hear Jason Gibson ride up with a cheery, "Hey there, Charlie." A moment later Mickey erupted through the back door, letting it slam shut behind him.

Next minute the younger kids streamed out in his wake, the screen door slamming again.

The rather interesting tension building between herself and Charlie abruptly shattered, Kat turned her attention to practical matters. Charlie Reynolds would keep.

Note to self. Get a soft-close catch fitted on that bloody door before that slamming drives me insane!

"And where do you lot think you're going?" She demanded of the four younger children. *Time to set a few ground rules.* "I hope you're not planning on getting in the way of my workmen."

"I was going to see if Luke can come round and see my room," Dennis muttered, vainly attempting to avoid his new-found sister's discerning eye.

"Before helping to clear up after breakfast? And have you all made your beds and tidied your rooms?"

Downcast eyes sliding away from hers answered her questions without need for further questioning.

"Come on. Work first, then you can all invite your mates over for lunch. I'll flash up the barbie. That includes you and Jason, Charlie. I'll be cooking hamburgers for everyone."

By the time Kat returned from laying in supplies to see them through until Maggie Bardon arrived to take charge of the housekeeping, the number of people expecting hamburgers for lunch had swelled to include Ailsa's friend Sonia Walsh and the twin's friends, Gwynna – who had changed her name from Smith to Lambert following her mother's marriage to Joey lambert – and Molly Tan.

"Good thing I bought double what I thought I needed," Kat laughed, glad of this earlier than expected opportunity to get to know the kids' friends. She suspected there'd be little time to spare once she began work on Monday. Curiosity alone would ensure a full surgery until the novelty of her presence wore off.

"Hey, Kat," Mickey stuck his head round the door shortly after. "Charlie says it's smoko time and wants to know if there's any chance of a coffee."

"Coming right up, Mick. Okay, kids, all hands on deck. First, wash hands, then Dennis, you and Luke find out how Charlie takes his coffee and what the boys want to drink. Girl gang," she turned to the gaggle of young girls, eliciting giggles at their new appellation, "put those biscuits I bought from Molly's mum onto a plate, please," she pointed to a cupboard, hoping she remembered where she'd stowed the serving platters the afternoon before, "and take them out to the table along with enough glasses for everyone. Ailsa and Sonia, do either of you know how to work this coffee machine? You do, Sonia? Thanks. You can make Charlie's coffee. Ailsa, can you take the juice out and start filling glasses, please?"

"Charlie says strong and black, no sugar and Jase and Mickey said they'll have juice."

"Okay. Got that Sonia?"

"So what are you gonna do, Kat?"

The cheek of the brat!

Kat cuffed him lightly, trying not to grin.

"I, Dennis, shall make myself a pot of tea. Here, don't leave empty-handed. You can carry out my cup and saucer."

"Yoo-hoo!"

Visitors? Groaning, Kat went to answer the quick pat-a-pan on the front door, finding Eddie Patterson standing there with a potted rose bush in each hand.

"Kat dear. I just popped round with these cuttings I struck from my bushes. They're cream banksia roses. Climbers. No thorns. I'm sure you'll find a spot for them. Millie Roberts told me you like roses."

An excuse to see what I'm up to, more like, Kat thought, burying her cynicism beneath a welcoming smile. She had Eddie's measure, and having detected the kind heart behind it, discovered she rather liked the older woman's blatant nosiness.

"Thank you, Eddie. They look nice and healthy and thornless is a plus. We're about to have a cuppa. Come and join us."

"Thank you, dear."

Taking the pots from her guest, Kat led the way through to the outdoor room. "Another cup for Ms Patterson, please Ailsa."

"Sure thing, Kat. Hello Aunt Eddie."

In no time at all the crunching of biscuits and the occasional slurp were the only sounds vying with the chatter of magpies working over the newly turned earth where Charlie and the boys had been digging postholes.

"So, Kat, what other plans do you have for the backyard?"

"Oh, we've got huge plans, Eddie. Haven't we kids?" Kat invited the children to join the conversation.

Nothing loath, Dennis accepted.

"We're getting a pool, Aunt Eddie. And chooks."

"And a playhouse," Estelle chimed in.

"It's not really a playhouse, Stelle," her twin amended, "It's a summerhouse. We have to share it with everyone else."

"Yeah, I know. But it will be mainly ours."

"Kat said I can have a lotus pond and a lavender patch and she's going to have a bush garden out front."

"Yeah, Ailsa," Dennis couldn't contain himself. "Your pond is going to be in the centre of my sundial with the gnumb... the pole thingy sticking up in the middle."

"That's gnomon, numbskull." Mickey corrected his brother with cheerful superiority.

"Yeah, whatever. It was my idea, though. All you could think of was a volleyball court and silly old vegetables. We're going to work out where to put the sundial numbers round the edge of the pond by watching the sun next month on the solstice day, Charlie. Sort of like a science experiment. Kat liked my idea best, didn't you Kat? You said I have an artistic soul."

"And so you do, Dennis," Kat laughed, stepping in to ward off a sibling spat by adding, "but everyone had tons of brilliant ideas. I'll just get the plan to show Charlie, and you, too, Eddie," she added, noticing both of them looking somewhat bemused.

"I'll get it." Shooting out of his chair, Dennis was half-way to the office for her sketchbook before Kat got to her feet.

Moments later the plan lay on the table with all five of the children crowding around, proudly pointing out the features they were responsible for to their friends.

Kat cheerfully took unfair advantage of the chaos by moving behind Charlie, leaning against his back, her arm draped casually over his shoulder as she leaned in to point out salient features. Now she'd had time to accustom herself to her body's physical reaction to his nearness, she decided she liked it. A lot. She felt she was waking from a long, lonely hibernation. The calculating question in Eddie Patterson's eye only made her smile all the wider as new energy flooded her system.

"You see," she explained when the kids' excited chatter slowed to let her get a word in edgeways, "it's not just my garden, my house. We all have a stake in it. It's *our* garden. *Our home*. I'll be giving you another list of plants, Charlie, and I'd appreciate your advice on a reliable watering system."

"Of course. Let me know what you want." With raging lust frying his brain, Charlie was amazed he'd managed even such a minimal response. Kat Murphy's curves pressing into his back, her subtle, spicy perfume clouding his brain, meant it was all he could do not to throw her down on the table and devour her.

It was a good thing there were kids present giving his saner instincts something to latch onto. Not to mention Eddie Patterson, The Crossing's answer to CNN. He scrambled to wrench back his self-control. It was no use him getting ideas. The woman was not for him. On top of everything else, he'd done a lightning costing of the projects she had planned plus what she'd already laid out. She must be loaded. Which only placed her even further out of his league.

"Boys," he croaked, not at all pleased with his unnaturally scratchy tone, "this is all very exciting and impressive, but there's still a job to be getting on with today."

He pushed his chair back, standing so abruptly Kat was lucky not to end up sprawled on the floor.

Biscuits and juice gone, the children soon vanished too, leaving Kat alone with Eddie.

"You've done a good thing for those children, Kat. It's long overdue for them to feel someone cares about them."

"They've had so little, it's hard not to shower them with too much all at once. I don't want to end up going overboard and spoiling them, but they need so much other kids take for granted. Every now and then I have a panic attack, wondering if I was totally insane to take on such a huge responsibility. It's good to know I can come to you for advice, Eddie. I reckon I'm going to need it."

"Anytime, Kat dear. Although, mind you, I reckon you've got the right stuff. Thanks for the cuppa, but I'd better be on my way. Mike will wonder where I've got off to."

As she walked Eddie out to the gate, Kat stopped where the veranda stepped down to the path.

"What do you think, Eddie? I could put your roses in big pots here and train them up on an arch framing the entrance."

Her head titled to one side, Eddie considered the image. "It'll look just lovely, Kat. Big dark blue pots, I think."

She stopped to think for a minute, then, decided she wouldn't be betraying a confidence.

"You know, Kat, I met another new resident of The Crossing the other day. Gillan Martel. Old Agatha Riley's granddaughter," she confided.

"She's a potter. She would probably appreciate me sending some business her way. It might be worth giving her a call if you want something special in the way of planters and pots for what's promising to be a rather spectacular garden. I'll text you her contact details."

Nothing like two birds with one stone, Eddie congratulated herself. *And isn't it nice the dynamics I observed between Kat Murphy and Charlie Reynolds last night really are just as interesting as I thought.* She headed for home imbued with the pleasant buzz of a morning well spent.

~~~~~

By the time Kat had made up the bed in Maggie Bardon's quarters, previously the Roberts' guest suite, and generally tidied up it was time to begin thinking about the promised burgers for lunch. Ailsa and Sonia reappeared from upstairs to give a hand, and Kat was surprised at how much fun the two girls were, with their chatter about movies and friends, and, especially from Sonia, boys. The more she saw of this sister of hers, the more she liked her.

The enticing aroma of grilling onions and meat, or maybe the growling of empty tummies, brought the younger children in shortly after.

"Lunch when you're ready, Charlie."

"Righto. Feed the kids first, then we'll be ready for a break."

Leaving it to her helpers to serve the children, Kat wandered out to inspect the work.

"Heck, Charlie, you're damn near finished! I'm impressed."
~~~~~

She let her seductive smile intimate she was impressed with more than his work ethic. The red tide creeping up his neck informed her she'd hit her mark.

"Still a lot to do. We've only got the fencing in place so far. Still got all the planting to go then I'll have to shape and tie the trees."

"Whatever. I'm still impressed with the progress." She couldn't resist giving his shoulder a pat as she walked past him. Somehow, touching Charlie, even as casually as that, reinforced her heightened sensation of being alive. Of having woken from a deep sleep. She chuckled from the sheer joy of feeling so good.

"Come and eat when you're ready, Charlie."

Fifteen minutes later when she turned from the servery with her own full plate, intending to sit next to Charlie as she had at smoko, Kat didn't know whether to be amused or chagrined to discover her target had a twin either side of him. The only spare chairs were at the opposite end of the table.

Running scared, Charlie Reynolds? Now why is that, I wonder? She was hardly a femme fatale, but Kat couldn't remember so blatant an invitation being turned down for no obvious reason.

So maybe there was a reason. Something in Charlie's background making him unwilling to get involved.

Or, and her heart sank, *he doesn't need a reason. He just isn't interested.*

In me.

Maybe there's someone else. Someone he loves. Maybe I'm imagining what I feel is mutual.

Kat reached for her glass, hoping the icy soft drink would cool the heat her thoughts generated in her cheeks. A few minutes later, making an effort to appear normal and avoid attracting adverse attention, she tuned back into the conversation.

"How come a nice man like you isn't married, Mr Reynolds?" a blushing Sonia was asking.

A question Kat could do with an answer to as well.

"Don't be so nosy, Son," Giggling, Ailsa elbowed her friend in the ribs. "Don't you know it's rude to ask personal questions?"

"How do ya find out if ya don't ask?" was Sonia's irrefutable response.

"You planning on taking over from Aunt Eddie as The Crossing's chief purveyor of news?"

A very expressive finger was all the answer Jason's comment earned, making everyone laugh. Even Charlie.

"Oh well, Sonia. Here's the scoop," Charlie shrugged. "It's no big secret. I used to be married, but we got divorced. Now I'm on my own."

"You're a decent man, Mr Reynolds. I bet it was her fault. Sorry I was so rude."

"That's okay, Sonia. You had a point, I guess, but sometimes people don't like talking about personal stuff." His uncomfortable shuffling made it clear Charlie was one of those people.

At that point, Dennis, bored with the conversation, snitched a cherry tomato from Clarice's plate and the ensuing rumpus effectively changed the topic.

Shortly after, Charlie led Mickey and Jase back to work.

While she put away the leftovers and stacked the dishwasher Kat mused on Charlie's admission. A divorce. Which might well have been acrimonious judging by his reluctance to talk about it. A divorce which might have left the man with a distrust of women. Could that be why he shied away from her? Despite his apparent physical attraction. She needed to think carefully about whether or not to continue teasing him. Needed to be sure of how far she wanted the flirtation to go. A bit of fun was one thing, being downright cruel another entirely. Her frustration at not having answers made her distinctly sympathetic with Sonia.

How did you find answers you wanted without asking?

Huffing to herself, Kat finished up in the kitchen and went out to cut roses from the front garden to brighten up the lounge room. Her house was rapidly acquiring the atmosphere of a real home.

She wandered idly round the side of the house to check out the planting, wondering if there'd be an opportunity for private conversation.

"What's that?" Startled, Kat turned in the direction of the siren warbling a screaming summons.

At almost the same time Charlie's phone chimed and he read the incoming text message.

"Fire callout. Gotta go."

He rapidly finished planting the tree he was dealing with and dusted his hands on the back of his jeans. "I'll be back when I can to finish up, Kat. Can the boys shove my gear in the shed out of the way? See you at the nursery tomorrow, boys."

Not waiting for an answer, he slammed the door of his ute and backed out.

Looking round, Kat observed a thin trail of smoke curling above the treetops. It looked to be a fair way off, but she shuddered, aware of the speed a fire could travel and the devastation it could carry in its wake. Thank goodness the wind was blowing away from the town. Turning aside, she bent to pick up the tools Charlie had flung down in his wake.

"Leave those, Kat," Mickey said, taking the spade from her hand. "We can finish the planting, can't we Jase? Then Charlie will only have to trim and tie. We'll put everything into the garage when we finish."

"Sure will Doc. We'll even tidy up the yard for you," Jason grinned winningly.

A heartbreaker in the making.

Kat waved acceptance with a wry smile and went to curl up with the latest Candice Fox novel on the front veranda.

<p style="text-align:center">~~~~~</p>

The fire had proved more ferocious than first expected, keeping the RFS, including Charlie, out for three days.

The boys had been as good as their word, finishing the planting and cleaning up. Maggie Bardon had taken up residence on Sunday, settling in as if she'd always been an integral member of their household, and Kat herself had officially begun work and was run off her feet.

It seemed an age since Kat had flirted with Charlie. In her quieter moments after dinner, she missed him.

He came on Wednesday to complete the job and collect his tools, but it was during the afternoon when she was up to her ears in patients at the Medical Centre across the street.

Was it merely coincidental, or did he deliberately avoid me? He could have phoned, and he hasn't done that, either.

Recalling his reluctance, Kat questioned herself and her feelings. Did she really want to risk getting involved with a man? Besides, nothing had actually happened, so why did accepting nothing ever would make her head hurt? To say nothing of her heart.

10

Kat immersed herself in work. And family. And tried to forget that for a few crazy days she'd almost believed there could be more. With a cheque to settle Charlie's account in the mail, she toughened up and consigned her brief idea of a relationship with him to oblivion.

She contracted the Gill brothers to begin work on her backyard landscaping, and the pool company promised to have them swimming by the end of January. It cost her another pang when she emailed Charlie the list of plants she wanted, and she wished there was another local supplier she could go to. But she stayed strong.

The kids were great. Funny and utterly loveable. It scared her how quickly she'd connected with them. Had grown to love them. Everything with the kids felt so right it warmed her heart. Until the evening Dennis – of course it was Dennis – accidently broke a glass in his usual rush to leave the table.

"Stop! Stand still!" Kat commanded in a sharp, authoritative voice the children hadn't heard before.

They froze where they were, staring fearfully at her. When she urgently pushed back her chair and stood, Dennis shook, the blood draining from his face. Instantaneously, she was cast back in time to a similar incident from her own childhood, only then it had been her father roaring at Sean that he was '…a bloody useless waste of space', one of his typically nasty verbal attacks followed immediately by a clout around the ears. Realisation struck. In her father's life Dennis had filled the position of scapegoat left vacant by Sean's disappearance.

Dennis expected her father's brand of retribution.

From her.

"You've got bare feet, Buddy," she said in a soft, matter-of-fact tone, her mind frantically processing what she'd learnt so unexpectedly. They all acted so normal she hadn't noticed the undercurrents. Or else she'd ignored them.

"There are shards of glass everywhere."

She picked Dennis up bodily and plonked him back onto his chair, silently cursing her father yet again.

"You stay put, Den, till I clear it all up. The last thing I want is to play doctor at home if you cut your feet. I get enough of that at work, you know."

"I'm s…s…sorry, Kat." A quickly swallowed sob caught in the boy's throat. He sagged in his chair, relieved, but not quite believing his luck. "I … I didn't mean to break it."

"Course you didn't." Kat reached out to ruffle his hair, cursing again under her breath when he flinched. "It was only a glass. No big deal. I bought extras knowing there'd be bound to be accidents."

She turned away to fetch the dustpan and brush only to find Maggie was ahead of her. In next to no time the floor was declared safe.

"Okay, Dennis. All clear. Off you go now." Kat waited till the boy was well away, then turned her attention to the other children, still sitting rigidly in their places, although they were now relaxing somewhat.

"So tell me, kids. How often did your father hit you?"

"How did you know he hit us?"

"Mickey, he was my father too, remember? I recognised the signs."

"He mostly left the rest of us alone," Ailsa told her. "Unless we were too slow dodging, then we'd get a quick backhander."

Kat felt sick. She knew from past experience exactly how hard Colin Murphy's backhanders were.

"That's right," Clarice added. "It was usually just Denny he hit."

"Yeah. He really picked on him a lot."

Because he is small and vulnerable

The perfect target for a bully like that bastard. Mick and Ailsa are big enough to strike back. Even in his drunken state he'd be wary of retaliation after Pat stood up to him, then me, and the twins were two against his one.

That bastard had so much more to answer for than I understood. Maybe I was a bit premature in thinking I'd forgiven him.

Now she understood more fully the extent of the damage he'd done to the kids, he could rot in Hell before she'd forgive him. There was absolutely no excuse for violence. Especially against kids.

"Stell's right," Mickey said, breaking in on Kat's dark musings. "For some reason he just seemed to have it in for Dennis. We used to do what we could to protect him, but …" He shrugged.

Kat drew in a deep, calming breath. There was nothing to be gained by losing her temper. Her father was dead, and the kids didn't deserve to be exposed to more scary behaviour.

"I'll talk to Dennis later, but just so you know, I don't hit. I don't believe in corporal punishment. If punishment is in order, we'll negotiate something reasonable."

Shortly after, dinner had been cleared away and the children had all disappeared upstairs intent on their own pursuits. Kat slumped down on the lounge, wondering if she had it in her to heal the damage done to these kids. Neglect was one aspect of abuse, but violence was something else again.

"Here, Kat." Maggie had come quietly into the lounge room, a tea tray in her hands. "I reckon you could do with this. For what it's worth, I think you handled the situation well."

"Oh Maggie. I felt so useless. I knew what the Old Man was, but I'd let myself ignore it. I shouldn't have. I should have realised everything was going too well."

"It was going well because you were doing right by those kids."

"I thought they trusted me, but Maggie, they were scared. Of me! All of them. That hurts."

"It wasn't really you, Kat. But I do think it's going to take time for them to genuinely trust any adult. No-one stepped up for them till you. That makes all the rest of us in The Crossing complicit to a greater or lesser degree for not noticing and doing something about it. And that was before you arrived on the scene."

Silence reigned for a moment. Thinking over Maggie's words, Kat poured a cup of tea, breathing the soothing scent of camomile and lavender deep into her lungs.

"You know, Kat. It's not my field, but I reckon the kids might benefit from counselling."

Maggie thrust her hands into the pockets of her apron, avoiding Kat's eyes. Some might say advising the doctor on childcare wasn't her place, but she was on the frontline with those kids. Everyday. She figured that made it very much her business, and she was prepared to defend her words.

Kat sipped her tea. Considering the idea.

"I reckon you could be right, Maggie. Leave it with me."

Kat noticed the other woman visibly relax.

"You know," she added, smiling, "I'm so glad Eddie introduced us. You're just who this family needs. Just who *I* need. Thanks, Maggie."

~~~~~

While life with the kids settled into a happy, pleasant routine, the practice was groaning under the strain, and with Christmas fast approaching, Kat feared she and Fiona would burn themselves out before New Year.
~~~~~

She'd believed after the first week or two the pace would slacken as the novelty of her presence wore off, but, the population having steadily increased in recent years, that hadn't happened. If anything, they were busier now than before.

The Shire Council, responsible for the management of the Medical Centre which included other visiting health professionals besides Kat and her full-time practice, had replaced Nancy Perdis's office assistant who'd retired when Doc Roberts left.

Grace Nwodo, a stately African woman who chose to wear her colourful traditional dress instead of the utilitarian Council uniform of navy skirt teamed with white shirt, was worth her considerable weight in gold in Nancy's opinion. But while the office now hummed along, Kat and Fiona usually had a backlog of grumbling patients still waiting past when it was time to take their break.

Today was no exception.

Careless of the room filled with curious locals, Kat let her frustration get the better of her.

"God, Nancy. This is bloody impossible. Haven't there been *any* replies to my ads for an assistant doctor? I thought if they knew they wouldn't be on their own here, *someone* would be willing to give us a go."

"Not a squeak, Kat. Sorry. Maybe just before Christmas is a bad time to recruit staff."

"Maybe I need to advertise overseas. I'm reluctant to do that, but I'm stretched too thin. We need a second doctor, and soon, or I'll have to start turning people away. I don't want to do that."

"I've been thinking. Have you considered a nurse practitioner?"

Fiona, escorting a patient from her treatment room, offered an idea she'd been turning over in her mind. "I'm just an ordinary nurse with no more than basic training. A nurse practitioner would be qualified to do a lot more than me, and with two of us, there'd be less pressure on you, Kat."

Kat tapped her pen against the paper Nancy had handed over for her signature at the start of the conversation.

"Excellent suggestion, Fiona. I'll draft an ad tonight and we'll get it in the papers tomorrow. Let's hope nurses are easier to recruit than doctors."

That evening at dinner, Kat ran the idea past Maggie.

"You know everyone for miles around, Maggie. Have you heard of any nurses looking to re-enter the workforce? I'd know good locals would stay, since they'd already be part of the community."

"Ooh. You've got me there, Kat. There's no-one I can think of off the top of my head. You'd better advertise just to cover your bases."

Half an hour later, refreshed by a good meal and an enlivening ginger and lemon infusion, Kat was piecing together what she hoped would be an ad attractive enough to inspire a positive response when the phone rang.

Oh God. Not a callout! Please.

Her "Dr Murphy. How can I help you?" was a wee bit terser than usual.

"Er, Dr Murphy? My name is Kyle Murray. I hope you don't think I'm out of line, calling you at home like this, but I've heard you're looking for an experienced nurse for your practice. If so, I'd be interested." The warm, deep, very masculine voice grew progressively more confidant.

Kat nearly dropped the phone. Trying not to sound overeager, she walked the young man, Kyle Murray, through the qualifications for the job, one by one. Fortunately, preparing the ad meant she had all the right questions to ask listed in front of her. She couldn't believe it. He sounded perfect.

There had to be a snag.

"So, Kyle. Why do you want to give up what sounds like a promising career in one of the top hospitals in Australia to be a practice nurse in Oxley Crossing? Do you even know where we are?"

He laughed.

"I know The Crossing well, Dr Murphy. My favourite aunt, Ada Murray, has lived there for ages. I loved visiting her and Uncle Kev when I was a kid."

Ada Murray! The penny dropped. *Now* Kat understood how Kyle down in Sydney knew of the job before she'd had time to advertise it. Ada had been waiting to see her this morning and had undoubtedly heard everything.

"As for the why, Doctor, you're right about the career bit, only my personal circumstances have changed. I've got a five-year-old son, Christopher. Kit. He used to live with his mum, but she was killed in a car accident last month. I'm struggling on my own here in Sydney. He needs me. I'm all he's got."

A sniff was clearly audible. Kat waited for Kyle to collect himself.

"Unfortunately, childcare doesn't fit well with hospital shift-work, so I decided to look for a job which allows me to work regular hours and be home with Kit every evening. Aunt Ada heard you needed someone and thought of me. She's willing to take on before and after school care so Kit will be with family. It's what I need right now."

"Umm. Sorry for your loss, Kyle. Okay. Email me your CV and references ASAP and I'll get back to you in the next day or so."

The documents arrived five minutes after they ended the call.

He must be eager!

If Kyle was eager, so was Kat. She read his CV, going online to confirm his qualifications were genuine, noting they were exactly as he'd told her. And, exactly what she needed. Before she went to bed she emailed the Director of Nursing, Ward Managers and medical consultant he offered as references. She'd wait for their answers, but she had a good feeling about Kyle Murray and slept well that night.

Next morning she waltzed into the surgery, smiling and humming.

"Good news, people. The ever-trusty Oxley Crossing grapevine has produced a candidate for our nursing position. His qualifications are good and one of his references has already checked out. Come and look." She was booting up her computer and opening the emails as they all piled in to lean over her shoulder.

"He? Did you say 'he', Kat?"

"I did, Nancy. Kyle Murray. Nephew of The Crossing's very own Ada Murray."

Fiona giggled. "I wonder what our patients will make of a male nurse."

"A very handsome young man he is, too," Grace purred, eyeing the photo attached to his CV. "The ladies will be queuing for appointments with him."

"I reckon some of the men might be relieved to have a bloke on the team as well," Fiona added. "They get a bit uptight having to discuss personal stuff with a mob of women."

"So why does a hotshot type like him want to come here? Sounds a bit suss to me."

They others nodded in agreement with Nancy's comment. Kat smiled widely and explained.

"Oh, the poor man," Grace sympathised. "He's doing the right thing. The Crossing is a good place. His little boy will be happy here for sure. Just like my boys are."

"So, you're all happy with Kyle's application?" Kat asked. "We all have to work together, so we need to be in agreement." Answered by their murmurs of assent, she continued, "I'll wait till I hear back from the other referees before I get back to him, but it looks promising."

Three days later Kyle Murray accepted the offer Kat made him, agreeing to begin work the following week.

He arrived early, walking through the door on Friday the eleventh of December just as the last patient was ushered out before lunch.

"Kyle Murray," he announced in the soft, warm baritone Kat was familiar with from their phone conversations. "I thought I'd introduce myself before starting on Monday."

"Oh my," Grace murmured in the background.

Kat had to agree. Taking in the 188 centimetres of sleek, toned muscle and bone topped by a face even more handsome than his photo, she grinned. She could have been looking at a model for GQ magazine. Kyle Murray was going to generate some serious fluttering among the young women in Oxley Crossing. He was already generating flutters among the women on her team.

When the flurry of greetings subsided, he drew forward the miniature version of himself wearing snazzy red and blue framed glasses, who'd been hovering at his back.

"This is Kit. My son." Love and pride resonated in every inch of him. "He wants to see where I'll be working."

"Welcome, Kit. I'm Dr Kat, and as you just heard us tell your dad, these ladies are Nurse Fiona, Ms Nancy and Ms Grace. Would you like to have a look around?"

Now what was so funny in that? Kat frowned at Grace who'd collapsed in a fit of giggles.

"Kit," her hapless office assistant spluttered. "And Kat. You and our boy here ought to team up for the best costume competition at our annual fancy-dress ball. You'd be sure-fire winners dressed in red with your names across your chests."

"Oh, a KitKat."

Now everyone was laughing, even young Kit when his father bent down to whisper in his ear.

"Does that mean we're chocolate buddies, Dr Kat," he said with an impish smile.

Even the son is a charmer. Look out Oxley Crossing.

Kat laughed, offering her hand. "It sure does. I'm proud to be the Kat to your Kit."

11

Kyle settled in quickly, proving to be not only popular and highly capable, but his adeptness in deflecting the attention generated by his dark, film-star good looks without giving offence, demonstrated a maturity beyond his years. Kat was barely accustomed to her lightened load when Christmas was upon them.

Maggie Bardon went home to spend the holiday with her family, but she left the fridge and pantry stocked to withstand a siege, and Bridget, John and their children came on a visit, laden with more cakes, jams and pickles along with two kittens, a box of cuttings for the garden and a dozen Isa Browns pullets to take up residence in Dennis's brand-new chook pen. All welcome additions to 'Murphy Farm', as Ailsa had dubbed their home.

With the house full to overflowing, it was Kat's happiest Christmas since her mother died. For the kids, it was simply the best Christmas ever, in spite of the wickedly hot, dry weather. There were a few grumbles and moans about 'why couldn't the pool have been installed earlier', but a slip-n-slide from Santa went a long way in compensation.

Kat had closed the surgery, rostering herself on call for emergencies only, giving Fiona and Kyle extra time with their families. She almost made it through the week without a call, but on New Year's Eve Fran Porteus sent for her.

The fierce westerlies had pushed the temperature to a record high, and a new flare-up of bushfires along the ridges kept the volunteer firefighters busy when they'd have much preferred to spend the time with family and friends.

Just on dusk the news was radioed through from the fire front. Two volunteers had been trapped and seriously injured when a burning tree fell on their truck. They'd been rescued and were being brought to the hospital for treatment. Kat was needed. Her pulse racing, and her breath coming in gasps, she ran across the street to the hospital.

What if it's Charlie?

She'd thought she had put him out of her mind.

It took only one hint of danger for her to realise he'd taken root in her heart as thoroughly as the orange trees he'd planted had taken root in her backyard. He might not want her, but she still wanted him. Only right now she had other, more urgent, considerations. Inside, she worked quickly to prepare the treatment room for whatever was coming their way. The sketchy information had included reports of a broken leg as well as serious burns.

All was in readiness when approaching sirens announced the arrival of the injured men under police escort. Kat, Fran and two more hospital nurses rushed into the carpark with gurneys to meet them.

Relief swept through Kat on seeing Charlie, filthy with ash and smoke, jump down from the driver's seat of the Landcruiser transporting their patients.

He had the back doors open by the time the gurneys were in position, someone inside sliding a stretcher forward towards him.

"Kat! This one first. Burns and a possible heart attack. I had the police radio for a helicopter to ship him out. The other guy can wait a bit."

"Kyle! What are you doing here?" Not that Kat waited for an answer. She was already examining the man she recognised as Andrew Morgan from *Morgan's Run*.

"He's been working on the first aid station out at the fire. Damn good bloke," Charlie said, helping Fran push the gurney while Kyle and one of the other nurses dealt with the less urgent Ted Lanner who had burns to his face and neck and a broken tibia.

It was touch and go for a while as Kat and Fran worked desperately to stabilise Andrew Morgan. He was responding to treatment when his wife, Barbara, fetched by Sergeant Matthews, dashed in from volunteering on the support crew catering meals for the firefighters.

"Where's my husband? Is he okay? Oh, Andrew, you stupid old fool," she cried, dashing tears from her eyes. "When will you learn to leave it to the young ones?"

He was too weak to answer, except to squeeze the hand which had clasped his, but it could be seen his wife's presence had given him strength.

The whump-whump of the helicopter landing on the flat paddock out the back of the hospital was the signal to move him out, and within minutes he was airborne, Barbara going with him. At the last moment she tossed her apron into Fran's arms, shouting something about being shipped off to Sydney with not even a toothbrush to her name.

Back inside there was a riot called Ted Lanner to be quelled, a task Fran Porteus waded into with relish.

"What's all this racket, Ted? Don't you know this is a hospital? We've got sick people here."

"Sorry Matron." Ted ducked his head, his belligerence suddenly turned into meek obedience. "It's just these blasted nurses saying they'll send me up to Tamworth in the ambulance. It's only a flamin' broken leg, fer gawd's sake. What sort of a hospital is this if you can't even manage to take care of a bloke's broken leg, then?"

"Humph! Doctor," Fran consulted Kat, "what do you think?"

"Let's have a closer look then, Ted."

"We've just ex-rayed the leg, Doctor." Nurse Mandy Jones showed Kat the X-ray.

"It's a clean break. I can set it, and I see your burns have been dressed. As for staying here, that's up to Matron. I don't make hospital policy." Grinning, Kat passed the buck straight back. As far as she could see there was no need to send the man away if he wanted to stay.

"Oh, alright then, but I know you, Ted Lanner. You'll do as you're told or it's straight off to Tamworth with you."

"Yes Matron."

It was hard to read Ted's expression beneath the dressings covering most of his face and neck, but Kat would bet it was sheepish.

It wasn't until late that night as she kicked aside her tangled sheets that Kat had time to consider how her feelings for Charlie Reynolds hadn't abated one iota.

If they wouldn't go away, and it seemed they wouldn't, she'd have to do something about them. Only this time she would think first and not rush her fences.

~~~~~

"Have you heard the latest?"

Fiona rushed into the medical centre kitchen where Nancy and Kat were gearing up for another busy day, steaming mugs in hands. Without waiting for an answer, she rushed on.

"You've heard about those horrific fires down south? Well, now ours is out, we've been asked to help, and Bart Gibson, he's our brigade chief, you know, Kat, he's rounded up a crew. They took the big truck and left for the staging post early this morning. They won't know till they get there where they'll be deployed."

"That'd be right," Nancy replied. "I heard fire crews from all over are streaming into the area. There are even some flying in from California. Your old stamping ground, Kat. One of those reciprocal agreements."

Just then, Kyle arrived, to be immediately besieged for answers. Laughing, he held his hands up in a plea for mercy.

"Ladies, I can't help you. I'm new, remember? I'm not even a brigade member. I don't know who went with Bart."
~~~~~

They dispersed soon after as patients began arriving. All day the news circled round and round in Kat's mind. Who went with Bart? How would they cope? The Crossing volunteers were expert in fighting fires in the local region, but from everything she'd been seeing on the news, the fires along the south coast were firestorms like nothing anyone had ever seen before. Uppermost among all the questions was, 'Did Charlie go?'.

At dinner that night she learned more when even for the kids, the fires were the main topic of conversation.

"Sonia was crying at school today," Ailsa said. "Her dad is one of our firefighters who's on his way to join in. Her and her mum are really worried."

"Probably needlessly," Maggie tried to reassure her. Ailsa herself was near tears thinking of her friend's distress. "Our Rural Fire Service may be volunteers, but they're very experienced and well trained."

"Charlie went, too," Mickey added. "Jase and I saw his foreman, George Brigden, in town this arvo. He's not expecting Charlie back till at least next week, so he was making sure we'd be available all weekend."

Now I know. He's put himself forward like a flaming hero.

~~~~~

They were well into January by the time Bart and his crew trailed home with stories of the horror the people down south had survived.

"We missed the worst of it. Were only in on the mopping up. Place was laid bare by the time we got a look in. Bloody well nothing left. Whole towns wiped out. Bush and farms gone."
~~~~~

Bart was holding forth to his mates down the pub.

"But the most impressive thing I saw, was the way those folks were picking themselves up and making plans to rebuild. Already! Fantastic community spirit. I reckon this year we ought to share some of the money we raise with the tug-of-war on Australia Day with those people."

Raised glasses and murmurs of agreement promised there'd be no opposition to that plan when the time came to allocate the funds.

Kat heard the fire crew were home and safe, however, there was neither sight nor sound of Charlie Reynolds. If not for the frequency of his name on Mickey's lips she could have imagined he'd packed up and shot through. She began to feel antsy, wondering if her feelings were real or if she was imagining something which didn't exist.

Bloody men! More trouble than they're worth most of the time.

~~~~~

"Do you mind if we talk while you eat?" Maggie slid a late lunch of quiche and salad in front of Kat, pulling out a chair for herself as she spoke. "I've been waiting a while for a few kid-free minutes to get something off my chest."

Kat looked up, eyes narrowed.

"Sounds serious. Do I need to be worried?"

"Not at all. It's just …" In spite of being prepared, Maggie suddenly found herself lost for words. "Look, Kat. At the Country Women's Association meeting last week your name came up."
~~~~~

She hastily warded of the acerbic comment she saw hovering on Kat's lips.

"Nothing bad," she assured Kat.

Salt of the earth and the backbone of many rural communities, the CWA ladies were as renowned for a good gossip as much as for the good work they carried out.

"Quite the contrary, in fact. They're behind you one hundred percent. It's just, …" Maggie stuck again.

"C'mon, Maggie. Spit it out. Whatever criticisms they've got, I can take it."

Maggie laughed. "Not criticism, Kat. They're worried about you. Your well-being. The long hours you work have been noted. Also, you have no social life. After what happened to Doc Roberts they're worried you'll burn out. Mental health is a big issue in the bush, as I'm sure I don't have to tell you, Kat." She smirked, adding, "I've been tasked with seeing you get out for a bit of fun and relaxation without the kids in tow. Of course, certain ladies interpret that as 'finding a man'," she finger quoted.

"And I'll bet I could accurately name that clique." Kat didn't care if her tone was a bit acerbic. Meddling old ducks. Then she shrugged and laughed. It wasn't Maggie's fault the dirty work had been landed on her. "I'll also bet they came up with a truck-load of suggestions."

"Course they did." Relieved to get off so easily, Maggie laughed with Kat and got up to retrieve a folder from the kitchen counter. "They prepared this for you. It's a list of every social, sporting or other event going on around town. There, I've done my bit."

Handing the folder across, Maggie recall one last item on her agenda.

"Oh, and Kat? If you want to go to the dance down the hall on Saturday, I'll stay on and babysit the mob."

"Actually," Kat flicked idly through the folder of notes, hiding her face, "I just might take you up on that."

Will Charlie Reynolds attend the monthly dance?

It was for charity, and not everyone who attended went there to dance. Some of them were simply doing their bit, so even a few antisocial types were regulars.

She still hadn't managed a face-to-face with her quarry. He'd dropped her plants off while she was at work. Again. So the brief glimpse when he brought Andrew and Ted in from the fire had been all she'd seen of him. Maybe the CWA ladies ought to set their sights on *him*.

Taking the folder with her, Kat headed back to work. The ladies might be meddlesome, but they were right. She did need to get out occasionally or she'd go stir-crazy. As predicted.

"Ladies, and gentleman," she grinned at Kyle, "I'm planning to get involved in a few things around town. Any suggestions on what, out of this lot, might suit me?" She spread the leaflets across the reception counter.

"Oh, there's the choir. My George and I are in that."

"Sorry Grace. I'm more of a bullfrog than a chorister."

"Tennis club?"

"Maybe. Definitely not hockey or basketball. Put the tennis club aside, then."

"Oh, look. Trivia. I used to play with a team down the pub." Kyle, a newcomer himself, was taking a keen interest in the social possibilities. "It's on tonight. I think I'll give Ada a call and see if she'll mind Kit for me. You reckon I'll be able to find a team to join?"

"Well, if you can't, Kyle, we can make our own. I love quizzes and mind games. See you there tonight. There, that's enough extra-curricular activities for me. Tuesday trivia at the Bowlo and Friday night tennis. And I believe there's a dance this Saturday as well. I'm in danger of becoming a social butterfly."

"Mum plays trivia," Fiona chipped in. "She was saying there's only her, Charlie Reynolds and Wal Piper left in her team since Maureen and Peter went to live near their daughter down on the coast."

Kat's ears pricked up. Now she was definitely joining trivia.

"She wanted me to go to make up the numbers," Fiona continued, "but it's not my thing. I'll ask if you two can join them."

"Thanks, Fiona. That'd be great."

Kat was glad Kyle answered Fiona. She was afraid of sounding too eager, and her colleagues were every bit as discerning as the CWA ladies. She texted Maggie to see if she was free to mind the horde, mentally reviewing her wardrobe for something to subtly wow Charlie Reynolds. When she closed the door of her surgery behind her she pumped air and jigged on the spot before booting up her computer in preparation for the afternoon patients.

12

The auditorium at the Bowling Club was surprisingly full when Kat stepped through the door with Kyle who'd jogged up the stairs mere seconds behind her.

"Welcome to Trivia, Kat. You too, Kyle." On the lookout for them, Poppy MacIntosh's warm welcome made up for Wal Piper's stern scowl and Charlie's terse nod.

"Poppy tells us you two want to play with us. Well, as last year's Grand Champions, our team has a reputation to maintain, ya know," Wal drawled, a twinkle belying his scowl, "so if you're not up to our exactin' standards, you'll be lookin' for another mob to join."

"Reckon we've got something to prove, then, haven't we Doc?"

Oozing confidence, Kyle elbowed Kat in the ribs and made a show of setting out a notebook and pen.

Across the table it was Charlie who was scowling now.

What's eating him? Is it me or Kyle he doesn't want? Probably me.

Only, as far as she could tell, his disapproval was not directed at her. Which only left Kyle.

Why? I thought he approved of him? Surely he didn't think … No. No way. That was not only utterly ridiculous but arrogantly presumptive of her to even think it, but what else was left?

Searching her bag for a notebook and pen of her own, Kat hide her face, stealing another covert glance at Charlie. Amused, she sat back, anticipating an entertaining, and maybe instructive, evening.

"Heard Andrew Morgan's doin' okay, Doc. Good thing this young fella's more than a pretty face. He did real good, takin' care of our blokes out at the fire."

Kyle's blush at Wal's approval betrayed his youth. Charlie's grunted assent set her lips twitching, but the others had their eyes on Wal who was still speaking.

"Hear you've joined the SES, though, Kyle. Those State Emergency Services blokes do a useful job, but you should've come to us. The Rural Fire Service can always use a good man, or lady," Wal nodded to Kat and Poppy, "who's got the right stuff."

"I would have, Wal, only I prefer mucking about in boats to chasing fires. But everyone pitches in when they're needed, don't they? So I'll be helping on the first aid station again next time you need me."

"Fair enough. Might lean on you to run a course for us during the winter when things are quiet. Our lot could do with a refresher in first aid."

Just then Phil Morris, the quizmaster, called the room to order and it was game on. At the interval Kat had time to look about her and exchange greetings with Tony, Marcia and Hazel Whitman who were teamed with Megan Armitage and Geni Wright at the next table.

Recognising a few other familiar faces around the room she smirked to herself imagining the positive feedback heading the way of the CWA ladies on their affirmative action.

"How about it, then, Wal?" Kat demanded at the end of the night. "Do you want us back next week, or should we look elsewhere?"

"We didn't win, but the 'Bright Sparks' only pipped us by a short nose. Charlie? Poppy? They in?"

Another grunted assent from Charlie, but Poppy was generous with her praise.

"Of course they're in, Wal Piper. As if it was ever in question. They contributed even more answers than I expected. I taught Kat, you know, so I knew how smart she is, and Fiona assured me Kyle would be useful. The rest of us are out of touch with all that pop culture stuff he knows."

"Some of us just aren't interested in that racket that passes for music these days."

"Which is exactly why Kyle is such an asset. Don't be such a stick-in-the-mud Charlie. People will think you're getting old if you go on like that."

Heaving his bulk up from his chair, Wal snickered. He poked Charlie in the ribs, but let Poppy have the last word.

"It's been a good night, but I'm off," Kat interjected. "Walk me to my car, Charlie? I've got a couple of landscaping questions for you."

"I popped in to see Maggie the other day," Poppy chipped in. "Your place is going to be a show-piece when it's finished, Kat."

"Maybe. That's not what it's about, though. I just want a place the kids and I can all enjoy. A place to call home."

Adroitly, Kat cut Charlie out of the melee of departing players and steered him towards the door with a quick wave goodnight to the others.

They were almost to her car when the discussion on pond plumbing petered out and Kat clasped Charlie's arm. Bringing him to a standstill, she faced him, serious and unsmiling.

"I didn't get you out here on your own to discuss plumbing, Charlie. I owe you an apology. When you were working at my place I was all over you like a rash. With absolutely no encouragement. I was out of line. It's just ..." The next bit was tricky and she took a moment to gauge the effect her apology was having. She'd decided to be completely honest and upfront with Charlie. There'd be no more pussyfooting around with neither of them knowing how the other felt. That way inevitably led to misunderstandings. Life was too short.

"The thing is, Charlie Reynolds, I've got the hots for you, and I thought ... hoped ... maybe it wasn't entirely one-sided."

"Me? But I thought ... You and Kyle Murray seemed pretty close tonight. All that nudging and high-fiving. I thought ..."

"Kyle?" Kat laughed.

So I was right. He was jealous.

While the only emotion showing on the outside was mild amusement, on the inside Kat was happy-dancing.

"Oh, Charlie," she leaned against him for a moment, enjoying the feel of his lean, muscular body against hers. "Flattering, but no. He's *so young,* and I'm not into cradle-snatching. He makes me feel positively middle-aged. Like his auntie. Or an older sister at least. It's you who turns me on, you idiot."

Sobering, Kat made space between them, crossing her arms in front of her, facing him. There was just enough light in this corner of the carpark to make out his shuttered expression.

"I know you might not feel the same, Charlie, and I can take it if you don't. I simply wanted to clear the air and ask if we can be friends. No strings. I love kids, but I'm not looking for marriage, babies or happy-ever-after, you know. That's not my scene. What I'd really like is to be your friend. And," she peeped up from beneath her lashes, "if we should end up as friends-with-benefits, well, I reckon that would be even better."

Charlie seemed lost for words. Kat gave him a moment to absorb her offer.

"It's not that I don't find you attractive, Kathleen. I do. Too much."

Kat's heart kicked up its pace at that reluctant 'too much'.

"But you see, I'm no good for you. No good for any woman."

Now her mood plummeted. This was so not what she'd hoped for.

"So," Kat let her words come slowly, "no benefits, then? How about the other half of the equation? Friends?"

"Okay," Charlie's breath huffed out as if he'd been holding it in. "I reckon I can be your friend, Kathleen."

With a self-derogatory "Yay!" accompanied by an exaggerated fist pump, Kat pulled Charlie's head down to plant a smacking kiss squarely on his lips. Letting him go almost immediately, she whirled about and strode the few remaining paces to her car.

"I like the way you call me Kathleen," she said, looking back over her shoulder as she buckled her seatbelt. "You're the only one who does, you know. And Charlie, if you ever change your mind about the benefits, the offer's still open. Goodnight!"

Deciding she'd given him plenty to think about, Kat drove off without looking back. As if his decision didn't matter to her, either way.

Ball's in your court, Charlie Reynolds.

It wasn't till later she began to wonder what he'd meant by saying he wasn't any good for her. Or any woman.

It has to be either medical or psychological, she concluded. *Whichever, I'll need to tread carefully until I understand the problem.*

She was good at making snap decisions. Had to be in her line of work. Unfortunately, as Kat knew to her cost, in her personal life it meant she also tended to rashly leap without looking. All too frequently with disappointing results; her disaster of a marriage being a prime example.

With Charlie Reynolds she had an uncomfortable feeling jumping in boots and all might also end in disaster.

So, I'll advance with caution.

13

Advancing with caution was all well and good, except that patience had never been Kat's forte.

On Saturday morning she gave up waiting for Charlie to make the next move. Briefly *Why bother?* flitted through her mind. So why did she?

Gut feeling he'll be worth it in the long run. Besides, I've never actively pursued a man before, never had to, and it's fun. Frustrating, but fun.

That made two good reasons to take the initiative. Kat picked up her phone.

"Hi Charlie. Kat here. Won't keep you long, but there's something I'd like to ask you."

She almost heard his silent groan down the line.

"I've been roped in for this dance tonight. The Powers That Be," *the CWA ladies*, she amended silently, "want me to put in an appearance."

Her own protesting groan was clearly audible.

"I can just imagine it, Charlie. One person after another will buttonhole me to tell me all about their bad back, or their gut-ache or crook knees. It's an occupational hazard. I ought to be used to it, and I am, but it gets a bit tedious when I'd rather be having fun."

"So, what do you expect me to do about it?" Charlie muttered when she paused for breath.

"Expect, nothing, Charlie. Hope …? Well, I was thinking a good friend, and we agreed we're friends, didn't we?"

"Yeah. I guess." Charlie didn't sound too sure, but Kat rolled on regardless.

"A good friend, Charlie, would be at that dance too. Not as a date or anything. I have to drive myself anyway in case I get called out to an emergency. You'd just have to be there, and if you noticed my eyes glazing over, you might rescue me by cutting in and claiming a dance. A good friend wouldn't mind that too much, would he Charlie? Anyway, think it over. See you. Hopefully tonight."

Charlie eyed his phone suspiciously, wondering if there was a hidden trap in Kat's simple request. All week her offer of friends-with-benefits had been circling in his mind.

Friends-with-benefits and no interest in marriage, babies or happy-ever-after. God, it tempted a man. Could any woman be that good?

That perfect?

In his experience they might say things like that at the beginning then turn around and accuse him of misleading them when …

He made a coffee and went to see how Mickey and Jase were handling the potting on he'd set them to. The sight of Mick Murphy triggered another line of thought.

Kathleen already had a pack of kids. Maybe they really were enough for her. She already had a place of her own which was shaping up to be the best address in Oxley Crossing. She had a housekeeper, Maggie Bardon, to take up the domestic slack. A lot of people might think she had a damn-near perfect set-up. A lot of people might wonder why she needed a man at all.

Did she really mean it when she said she wanted none of the usual from him?

By the time he locked the nursery gates for the night, he was no closer to an answer. And there wouldn't be one, unless he took the plunge.

What did he have to lose? A bit of pride perhaps, but if Kathleen Murphy was as good as her word, he had an awful lot to gain. The stirring in his groin thinking of what 'benefits' might come his way pushed him over the line.

Into the shower.

Into decent casuals.

Through the door of the Community Hall.

~~~~~

"Charlie Reynolds! As I live and breathe." Incredulous, Hazel Whitman, guarding the door with her bestie Dot James drawled out her exclamation.

"It's so nice to see you taking an interest, Charlie." Dot was kinder. "Have a lovely time."
~~~~~

"And don't forget to dance, since that's the purpose of this event."

Escaping the dragons at the door, Charlie went in search of a familiar face or two, discovering Megan and Jon Armitage chatting with Geni and Ben Wright.

"Hey Charlie. Given up on hiding out from the ladies, have you?" Jon challenged with a grin.

Geni snickered behind her husband's back. Charlie's reclusive habits had been the butt of quite a few jokes since he'd taken up residence on his grandfather's old farm.

"You're lucky Eddie's babysitting or she'd have you matched up in a heartbeat."

Charlie shuddered. He'd had a run-in or two with Eddie Patterson and her cronies. Maybe this wasn't such a hot idea after all. He was gauging his chances of making a run for it when Kathleen entered, laughing at something Joey Lambert was whispering in her ear.

Joey Lambert's married, with his pretty young wife on his arm. What's he doing making up to Kathleen Murphy?

Silently smouldering, Charlie lightened up when the woman he was focused on waved off her companions to take the floor with Tom Carey.

"Can't a looker like the Doc find someone better to dance with than that ancient reprobate?"

"Apparently not, Ben," Jon chuckled. "There's a bit of a mystery there, but according to Mike and Eddie it seems they're old mates from back in the dark ages."

"Less of that 'dark ages' talk, thank you Husband-of-mine. I was at school with her, let me remind you." Megan elbowed Jon in the ribs, then led him out onto the floor, Geni and Ben following them. Left to his own devices, Charlie went to prop up the wall next to Wal Piper till the set came to an end.

"Didn't know you were a dancer, mate."

"I'm not, Wal. Just thought it was high time I did my bit to support the local fundraiser. Probably won't stay long."

"Don't see our pretty boy, Kyle Murray here. Reckon the girls will be spitting chips. Look at them, all dressed up and only us old codgers to show off to."

"Give over with the 'old codger', Mate. I'm only just forty, you know."

"Then stop acting like one." Wal was unrepentant, enjoying getting under Charlie's skin. "Get out there on the dance floor and show us what you're made of. There's my missus waving at me. We'll show you how it's done."

"Don't bloody need any showing," Charlie, on his own again, muttered under his breath, looking round for a partner. Kat was already being sedately steered round the floor by Bill Whitman, so he ambled over to the group of women chatting near the side door. The sight of freedom so close at hand tempted him to bolt, but that would be the coward's way out, so he nodded to Sally Gill and invited her to dance.

For the next hour he worked his way through the ranks of older women. Safe women.

He gave the younger set a wide berth. Too many jealous husbands and aspiring brides among that lot for his comfort.

Between sets he kept a surreptitious eye on the Doc who seemed to be holding her own with ease. Until she wasn't.

Dan Elliot had her bailed up in the corner, bending her ear. Charlie reckoned her eyes were glazing over. His cue. He brightened. He'd waited long enough. It was the Doc who was responsible for his being there and it was high time he made a move.

"Kathleen. Dan." He nodded a curt greeting. "Mind if I cut in, Mate? You promised me a dance, Kathleen, and a nice slow one's just starting if your feet are up to it."

"Nothing wrong with my feet, Reynolds," Kat tossed him a smile he read as grateful. "Lead the way. Nice chatting, Dan. If you're still worried, make an appointment on Monday."

"Phew, Charlie," she grinned. "I never knew there were so many bad backs in The Crossing. How come you took so long rescuing me? I've been sending you signals for ages."

"You didn't look to be in need of rescue till Dan buttonholed you."

Charlie breathed in her heady floral perfume and tightened his arm around her waist, pulling her in close against his chest. It felt right to have Kathleen Murphy in his arms. So right he had to wonder why he'd taken so long to get her there.

The music ended too soon. Charlie strung the moment out with an offer of refreshments, only they were soon caught up with a crowd and next thing he was trying to shake Tom Carey off, watching helplessly as the Doc was steered back to the dancefloor by Ben Wright. He didn't get a look-in again, and suddenly it was the last dance.

Now or never.

He muscled in, beating James Pritchard by a short head to secure the last waltz, nestling his Kathleen, realising that's who she was now, *his* Kathleen, in his mind at least, back into his arms.

Two dances.

Kat had hoped for more. She wasn't sure if Charlie had only asked her twice because he wasn't interested in more or because he hadn't tried hard enough. She'd told him what happened between them was up to him, but she'd hoped for more enthusiasm on his part.

Maybe he was put off by the attention his unaccustomed appearance generated.

Until overhearing snippets of gossip tonight she hadn't realised how reclusive he'd been. She snuggled closer, resting her head on his shoulder. Though the ball might be in his court, there was no reason she couldn't give him a bit of encouragement.

In the scramble to collect jackets and bags and head out the door for a fast getaway, Kat looped her arm through Charlie's and dawdled over her goodnights. Nothing loath, her escort anchored her hand against his flank and dawdled along with her, sauntering across to where her car was parked in a pool of shadows under a sheltering jacaranda.

With a lopsided smile, Kat thanked Charlie for his earlier rescue duties, then, throwing caution to the wind, rose on her toes to claim his mouth. It was meant to be another quick, 'friendly' kiss.

It wasn't.

This time Charlie was all in. An eager participant. His arms once again circled Kat's waist. Heat flared, overpowering thought. Sinking deeper, Kat revelled in the passion threatening to blaze out of control.

A piercing wolf-whistle echoed across the almost empty carpark.

Abruptly Charlie's arms fell away. He wrenched his lips free, twisting to look over his shoulder, cursing under his breath in words no true gentleman would ever utter in the presence of a lady.

Bloody Wal Piper!

Caught in the headlights, Charlie responded with a well-recognised gesture indicating his opinion. Ribald laughter floated on the breeze as Wal drove off, his wife berating him in her carrying voice.

Romance fled.

Kat collapsed into the driver's seat of her car in a fit of giggles.

Not my finest moment.

She hoped Wal kept his mouth shut. She'd been hoping to fly below the radar in her pursuit of Charlie Reynolds.

Pulling the door closed, she leaned out the open window calling, "Goodnight Charlie." She started the car and put it in gear.

Silently cursing himself, Charlie leant down for an awkward kiss through the window, but the mood was lost. He straightened, giving a half wave as Kat drove off.

The gods were definitely against him.

Charlie imagined their derisive sneers. He was out of practice in the dating game, but if he hoped to get anywhere with his Kathleen he was going to have to get up to speed. Fast. Before she wrote him off as a lost cause.

A little strategic planning was called for.

14

Charlie's idea of strategic planning meant finding a way to cut Kathleen free of the crowd and get her to himself. Unseen. Unobserved. In private. Fretting with impatience, it didn't take him long to make his move.

"Hey, Kathleen."

Kat smiled to herself on hearing the voice which had been in her dreams lately greeting her from her phone. But the dinner table was no place for an intimate chat.

"Excuse me, Maggie. Kids. I'll take this call upstairs."

Charlie heard the clatter of footsteps, then the click of a door closing. Finally, Kat spoke to him.

"You still there, Charlie? Your call came at just the right moment to get me out of kitchen duty. You coming tonight?" It was Tuesday. Trivia night.

"Actually, Kathleen, that's what I'm calling about."

Kat's heart sank.

But only momentarily, as Charlie continued.

"Would you mind giving me a lift? I've got transport problems, and I'd hate to let the team down."

"Well, we couldn't have that, could we? I'll pick you up in half an hour."

"Right. Thanks." Charlie was relieved when Kat hung up without querying his mythical 'transport problems'. Or expecting him to engage in small talk. There was a spring in his step as he tidied his kitchen and rechecked the pristine state of his bedroom. Dirty laundry in the basket. Flat surfaces dusted. Bed made with military precision. Clean sheets. The necessary in the top drawer, there being more than one reason to use protection.

Just in case.

Because, if his plan worked out, Kathleen would be giving him a lift home tonight. And, if he was lucky … He had trouble tearing his mind away from her promise of benefits. Now he just had to hope there wasn't a medical emergency to throw a spanner in the works.

Kat's brisk friendliness when she picked him up, a brisk friendliness bordering on the impersonal, continued throughout the evening. Charlie began to wonder if he'd somehow misinterpreted her offer of 'friends-with-benefits', although how? It was a pretty unambiguous euphemism for a no-strings sexual relationship, after all. Maybe she'd fallen back on a woman's prerogative and changed her mind.

Well, if she's that fickle, I'm glad I found out before I got in any deeper!

By the time they said their goodnights, Charlie's mood couldn't be called surly.

Not exactly.

However, a chip the size of a blackbutt log on his shoulder was apparent to others besides Kat. Even their team's narrow win didn't sweeten him noticeably.

"Bloody Hell, Mate. Get over yerself, will ya?" Wal punched him playfully in the arm. "Trouble in Paradise, is it? Stop actin' as if ya lost a dollar and found five cents. We won, Mate. We oughta celebrate."

"Love to, Wal," but I've got a patient to look in on after I get our miserable friend home." Once again, Kat adroitly cut Charlie out of the pack and steered him across the carpark.

"You mad at me, or something, Charlie?" she asked as they rolled out the gate.

"What makes you think I'm mad at you, Kathleen?"

"Oh, I don't know. Maybe that acerbic tone you used just now. Or maybe it's the way you've been cold-shouldering me all night? You tell me, Charlie."

"Maybe I just don't appreciate the way you lead me on one minute then change your mind the next," he growled.

"Changed my mind? Not me, Charlie. But my business is my own, and after catching us in the headlights Saturday night, I reckoned Wal would be on top of any overt sign of something going on between us."

She chuckled.

"I'm right, aren't I? You heard his 'Trouble in Paradise?' quip."

They were driving into the nursery before either spoke again. While Charlie mulled over her reply, Kat let him stew.

"I've not only *not* changed my mind, Reynolds, I'm hoping for an invitation for coffee. Or something."

"Of course! Naturally you can have a coffee. If that's what you want."

Seeing Charlie straighten in his seat, smiling for the first time since she'd picked him up that evening, brought a grin to Kat's face. One she deliberately wiped off a second later as she stepped out of the car, and, joining him at the foot of the steps, turned to face him.

"Before I set foot inside your house, Reynolds, let's get a few things perfectly clear, so there's no misunderstandings between us down the track. As I said, my business is my own. I don't want to hear the gossipmongers linking our names, blowing up a very simple arrangement into the latest Crossing romance. No strings. No talk. We're both exclusive for as long as whatever this is lasts. And, if either of us wants to call it quits, we say so and that's it. Respect on both sides, and no recriminations later."

She held her hand out.

"Deal?"

Strewth! That puts me in my place, good and proper!

Charlie wasn't used to such plain speaking from a woman, but it took only a second to realise his Kathleen's offer was precisely what he'd had in mind all along. *So why am I even thinking about it?*

"Deal!"

Charlie smacked his hand into hers, closing his fist around it and hauling her into his arms to seal the deal more appropriately than with a handshake.

The kiss went on. And on. It lit a fire in Kat's blood, and turned her knees to jelly.

"What are we doing, outside here with the possums and owls, Reynolds?" she murmured when they finally came up for air. Right on cue an owl hooted on the hill above the house. "Take me inside, Charlie," she giggled, "and there's no need to bother with coffee. I'm in the mood to see if you're as good in bed as your kisses promise."

"What? You're planning on giving me a performance rating?"

Kat giggled again. "There's an idea. Maybe I will."

Some considerable time later, back in her own bed, alone, she reflected that if a rating was asked for, she'd have to give Charlie Reynolds a resounding one hundred and ten percent. Plus.

She hadn't been expecting anything more than mere mutual satisfaction, so had been pleasantly surprised. Very pleasantly. Having a man put her needs and satisfaction before his own was an experience she could get used to. Would like to get used to. His stamina rating was also way above average. Kat smiled sleepily, her own hand sliding over her skin mirroring her lover's earlier caresses.

A man who didn't simply roll over and go to sleep after he came, but took the time to bring her down gently, then build her up to a new high better than the first, was another new experience she would very much like to get used to.

Could be this little fling might last longer than anticipated. Charlie Reynolds had the makings of a long-term lover. A keeper. Sleep overtook Kat before she took that thought any further.

Over the next few weeks, Kat and Charlie snatched greedily at any spare moments they could free up in their busy schedules, and, in Kat's mind at least, their relationship was all she'd hoped it might be. Mutually satisfying. Under the radar. And, best of all, no strings.

15

If only the nightly news on Kat's television had been as pleasant as her personal life she would have been on a perpetual high. Unfortunately, catastrophic bushfires, terrible enough, were chased from top billing by truly horrifying footage of a new disease in China.

Who'd ever heard of Wuhan? Overnight, it became the most talked-about city in the world, as viewers were confronted with images of people collapsing on the streets. And then it wasn't just China struggling to contain a disease no-one knew how to treat, let alone cure.

Dr Kathleen Murphy was chilled to the bone when reports poured in of the coronavirus spreading, with frightening rapidity, to other countries around the World. At the risk of being labelled an alarmist, she consulted with her team and ordered more of everything they thought they might need, hoping against hope they wouldn't.

Then Australia was on the front line, with a shipload of Australian tourists being carried off the *Diamond Princess* in Japan.

When her sister ship, the *Ruby Princess*, docked in Sydney, sending ashore both passengers and the disease, there was no more avoiding the issue.

Australia went into lockdown.

Wash hands, wear masks and stay at home were the orders; and the police enforced them.

Overnight, society changed. Business meetings were conducted using Zoom as most people worked from home. Children studied at home. Restaurants became take-away only and phone consultations with one's doctor became the norm unless a face-to-face meeting was deemed essential.

Even in Oxley Crossing, where Council and the local branch of the CWA resorted to Zoom meetings.

"Why can't we go to school?" Dennis whined, when Kat checked he'd completed the work his teacher set her class. "Luke and I had plans."

"No-one's sick in The Crossing, so why do we have to be in lockdown?"

Even sensible, level-headed Ailsa was becoming irritable and hard to live with and Kat's explanations of the use of containment to manage the disease everyone now called COVID-19 only led to more grumbles and moans. Losing patience, she gave them all an extra homework assignment.

"Clarice, Estelle, Dennis, Ailsa and you, too, Mickey," she glared around the dinner table at all of them.

"When you leave the table, I want you, all of you, to go on-line and research the story of what happened in an English village called Eyam. That's E. Y. A. M."

Kat hoped they'd get the point. She'd had enough of their whining about how hard they had it.

"We'll discuss your findings tomorrow night. Now, not another word about how awful *your* miserable lives are."

"Oh, Maggie, I'm so glad you stayed in town with us. I'd have strangled one of them by now if I'd had to cope with the kids alone on top of my work." Kat heaved a sigh of relief.

"That's my job, Kat," Maggie murmured. "Although, I must say, that pool I thought an unnecessary extravagance has helped safeguard my sanity."

Kat laughed.

"Kat, the village you told them to research? Is it the one they call the plague village?" Kat nodded. "I read a story about it."

"I've been thinking about it a lot just lately. Fourteen months in *voluntary* lockdown, so they wouldn't spread the Black Death to their families and neighbours. Do you reckon modern people could do that? Be that unselfish?"

Maggie shuddered. "I just hope and pray it doesn't come to that! Gran's stories about the Spanish Flu in 1920 were bad enough. I'm not sure this modern generation with their 'Me, me, me' attitude care enough, to tell the truth."

"Umm. I think they might surprise us, Maggie."

"Maybe. Anyway, I'm off to catch *Gardening Australia* on the tele. See you in the morning, Kat."

~~~~~
~~~~~

Early morning after a late-night call-out to the hospital was Kat's favourite time to visit her mother's grave. Her one-way conversations with Monica over the births, deaths and serious illnesses of her patients helped her immeasurably in ways she couldn't easily express, but which meant she didn't carry the dark moments of her work home to the children.

She was there once again, mourning the passing of one of the residents of the Steedman Wing. Archie Muldoon's passing had been long expected and quite gentle, but in the enforced absence of his family, Kat had sat holding his hand till his breath stilled. In the peaceful, scented dawn in the cemetery she felt the tension drain from her, body and soul. With a final murmured goodbye to Monica, she rose stiffly to her feet. Turning, she observed without surprise that she was no longer alone.

Charlie Reynolds straightened from his slouch against a towering headstone enumerating several generations of Whitmans.

"Charlie, fancy meeting you here." Kat's smile expressed a warmth her simple greeting left unspoken. She walked across, straight into his open arms, laying her head on his shoulder a moment before lifting her face to receive his kiss.

"Umm. Charlie," she whispered. "I've missed you. Damn this lockdown for keeping us apart."

"Me too. Missed you, I mean. Pity we're both such law-abiding citizens."

To their mutual satisfaction, they spent the next little while making the most of their unexpected encounter. Passion had risen to fever pitch before Charlie gently moved Kathleen out of their close embrace.

She sighed. "Here we are carrying on like a couple of randy teenagers. In the Dead Centre." She giggled. "Lousy timing, Charlie. I've got to be heading home to breakfast with the kids."

"Wish I was," Charlie grumbled. "You're lucky, Kathleen. I'd have given anything to have a family."

"You can share my lot anytime," she answered carelessly. "Maggie and I have about had enough of this home-schooling gig."

"Do ya really mean that?"

Kat stared, rendered speechless by his intensity.

"Because I've been thinking. Plenty of time for that lately. And what I think is, Kathleen, we're a pair of idiots to let what others say dictate our lives. We could have been together during this lockdown instead of shut away in separate houses. Just think of it. Together in the same bed, every night, all night. No leaving before dawn. Waking up next to each other every morning. I could have been there, helping you and Maggie with the kids, Kathleen."

Kat moved a couple of steps away, eyeing Charlie suspiciously.

"That wasn't our agreement, Charlie. No strings, remember?"

"I remember, Kathleen, but I wasn't in love with you then. Leastways, I didn't know I was."

Kat sucked in a breath, opening her mouth to refute his declaration, to be silenced by Charlie laying a finger across her lips.

"Hear me out. Please, Kathleen," he whispered.

Reluctantly, she nodded, crossing her arms over her chest, lips pressed tightly together.

This isn't going well.

Charlie took in his lover's aggressive stance, gulped, and carried on, determined to finish what he had to say.

"I love you," he reiterated. "Never thought I'd be saying that to anyone again, ever, but there it is." He shrugged. "I love you, Kathleen Murphy. It's not just the sex, which is great, by the way, it's the woman you are. Caring. Compassionate. Willing to do whatever it takes. Putting duty before pleasure. I like the quiet moments when we feel completely in tune as well as when we're having fun. I want to spend my life with you, Kathleen. I want to marry you."

The silence which met his final statement was loud enough to be heard as far away as One Tree Hill. Kat wasn't often lost for words, but on this occasion her mind was a total blank. Her vocal cords were frozen in her throat. When she finally forced sound from between her lips it was a strangled cry of frustration.

"Aargh! Bloody Hell, Reynolds. What do mean, changing the rules like this? What happened to no strings?"

Not quite the reception Charlie felt a proposal of marriage warranted.

"The agreement allowed us to change our minds, as long as we told the other up front. I'm telling you now. I love you. I want to marry you." Perhaps if he repeated the words often enough his stubborn woman would listen. Although right this minute, that seemed a far-off likelihood.

Now Charlie's arms were folded across his chest, his stance every bit as aggressively defensive as Kat's. An onlooker could be forgiven for imagining a blazing row was taking place.

"Damn you, Reynolds," Kat's curse was low and bitter. "I thought I was safe with you, then you go and pull a stunt like this."

Wheeling about, she strode across the graveyard in a beeline for her car. Startled, Charlie was slower to move, catching her just in time to hold the driver's door open and lean in.

"We don't have to change anything if you don't want to, Kathleen. We can carry on the same as before for as long as you like. Just promise me you'll think about what I said. Please."

Their eyes locked for a long, long moment during which the outcome hung in the balance. Kat huffed out a breath, slumping down in her seat.

"You're fooling yourself, Charlie, if you think we can blithely go on as before. You've changed everything. Everything. You can't unsay what you said, and I can't help thinking about it, can I? I'll ring you when I figure it out."

Defeated, Charlie stepped back. Kat slammed the door shut. Spinning her wheels in the gravel, she headed out of the carpark as if the hounds of Hell were on her tail. Several hours later, dating a prescription for Mike Patterson, she read the date again. Wednesday the first of April. April Fools' Day. And, oh boy, was the joke on her!

16

The week leading up to Easter, with its promise of an easing of COVID restrictions, was a long one for Kat, stewing over what she interpreted as Charlie's betrayal of their perfectly fine working arrangement. Why in Hell would any sane man want to change something so much to his advantage? Why did she have to get involved with the one man who did? She tried not to take her bad mood out on her family, friends or patients, but there was more than one muttered complaint about her lower than usual tolerance of minor annoyances.

It was an even longer week for Charlie, brooding over stuffing up his relationship with Kathleen Murphy. Who'd have thought she'd be so anti marriage? So unlike other women who, in his experience, were all eager for that march down the aisle? Why did he have to fall for the one woman who wasn't? It made a man wonder. It really did.

One person who, completely bound up in his own pursuits, wasn't bothered by any tenseness in the atmosphere was Dennis Murphy. He and Luke Whitman were off on their bikes every afternoon.

Exercising, they pertly claimed, while actually they were intent on some mysterious project for school. Any other week Kat would have found her little brother's angelic demeanour suspicious, and paid attention. This week she had other, more personal concerns distracting her.

Until Good Friday when Marcia Whitman phoned late in the afternoon.

"Hi Kat. Marcia here. Would you mind giving Luke a reminder to get himself home? We're going out to the farm for dinner with my parents and he promised to be home early."

"But Marcia, …" Kat was already on her way out to the pool, but she was pretty sure neither Luke nor Dennis was there. "You know, Marcia, I thought they were both at your place, working on their project. Dennis packed lunch and told me they were going for a picnic in the park, then back to yours."

"The little buggers! I'll skin Lukey alive when I get a hold of him. He told me the same story, except they were going to your place to swim."

Panic began to creep into Marcia's voice.

"They've been gone all day. Where do you reckon they might've gone, Kat? What are they up to? Do you think something's happened to them?"

"No idea, Marcia," Kat answered, her mind throwing up way too many possibilities she'd prefer not to give voice to.

"Give me a few minutes to ask the others what they know. I'll get back to you."

"Yeah. I'll talk to Jeremy. He might know what his brother's up to."

An hour later both homes had been thoroughly searched, along with Bill and Hazel Whitman's home; all siblings and close friends questioned; all the parks in town scoured from end to end. The two boys were definitely AWOL, and since they hadn't been sighted since Pete Hackett passed them on their bikes on Woodcock's Road early that morning, they could be anywhere.

Anything could have happened to them.

Sergeant Matthews was organising search parties when Tom Carey arrived, huffing and wheezing.

"Sarge," he gasped. "I've got an idea where those kids might be."

Everyone within earshot crowded around him, commenting and questioning until no-one could hear themselves think.

"Quiet! Now, Tom, get your breath back, Mate, and tell us what you know," the sergeant ordered, pressing the old bloke into the chair Kat passed to him.

"Well," Tom began, abashed at being the centre of attention, "I don't actually know anything. Not for sure, but I reckon it's that school project they was workin' on. You know, the local history thing. They were around asking me questions the other afternoon. Interviewing me like."

He smirked at his rapt audience.

"Apparently there's a prize for the most original presentation, and they wanted to win. It was all hush-hush so no-one else would pinch their idea, but they came to me to help with their map, since they didn't know where it was. I heard them whisperin' something about checking it out over Easter."

"Where what was, Tom?" Tony Whitman butted in. "What are you on about, man? I just want my kid home safe. And young Murphy. If you know where they are, just say so."

"I'm tellin' ya, aren't I? Stop bein' so damned impatient, Tony."

"Cut to the chase, Tom. Where do you reckon they went?" Don Matthews calmed the anxious father and tried to hurry Tom along.

"Thunderbolt's Cave. That's what their project was all about. That time Captain Thunderbolt hid out over here when the troopers made life too hot for him in his usual stampin' ground over Uralla way."

"Thunderbolt!"

"That old yarn?"

"Load of hogwash. He was never anywhere near here."

"Was too. What would a newcomer like you know?"

A cacophony of comments broke out again. This time the racket was even harder to quell, and Don gave up, leaning close to speak to the old man.

"Can you show me the cave on the map. Tom?"

"Better than that, Sarge. I can take you right there. Up in the National Park it is. Just follow the fire trails up the valley to that big limestone bluff above the wide bend in Dead Horse Creek."

"Right! Listen up you lot," Don bellowed. "Tom and I will take a look at this cave, then radio back instructions."

He turned to his senior constable.

"Madden, I'll keep in radio contact so you know what's happening. If we don't find them, send out the search parties as planned. Doc, you better come along too, in case there's been an accident."

Moments later, with Don at the wheel and Tony Whitman insisting on riding shotgun, Kat found herself wedged into the back seat of the sergeant's 4x4 truck alongside Tom Carey.

"Gee, Lass. I sure hope we find them," he said, squeezing her hand.

"Me too, Tom."

At a soft patch along the rutted trail, Don and Tony got out to examine bike tracks in the dust.

"They're fresh. Looks like you could be right, Tom," Tony reported. He was looking grim, unwilling to speculate further.

While it would have taken the boys on their bikes two hours at least, the rescue party took only minutes to cover the same ground. Two bikes propped against an old river red gum proved Tom right. Don pulled into the small clearing beside the creek and parked alongside them. He laid on the horn. A good long blast followed by a couple more, all of which elicited no response beyond setting a flock of sulphur-crested cockatoos wheeling and screeching above the creek.

"Looks like they're inside. Come on."

Their way lit by Don's police issue torch, the four of them inspected the inside of the deep overhang, calling out to the boys as they went. When no answer ensued, despite evidence the boys had been there, Tom led the way to a narrow fissure in the back of the cave.

"I told them how the cave goes back a ways into the side of the hill," he said. "I bet those two have gone exploring."

Kat groaned. She bet they had, too. How could an enterprising pair like Luke and Dennis have passed up such an adventure. She hated caves, but trailed after the men.

"At least they showed some common sense." Don reached down to check a string tied to a heavy rock placed at the entrance to yet another narrow passage branching off from the inner chamber. He pulled on it, but there was no answering tug. "Any idea what's through here, Tom?"

"Nah. Sorry. It gets pretty rough and squeezy in there and without proper equipment none of my mates were game to risk it. We could hear water dripping, and it was wet underfoot. Probably a good thing there's been no rain the last few weeks."

"Luke! Luke! Where are you?" Tony was about to follow the stringline in search of his boy, but Don pulled him back.

"They're not answering, Tony. They must have gone too far in to hear."

He was careful not to voice the other reason for their silence, though it was most likely what they were all thinking.

"I'm going back to radio for help. We'll do the boys no good if we go barging in and end up in a jam ourselves. I for one am not built for squeezing through the back-end of a cave with just one torch between the four of us. That'd be asking for trouble."

None of them liked it, but waiting for a rescue team properly equipped to go deep into the unexplored cave system made sense.

While they waited, they continued to call at intervals.

Once Kat could have sworn she heard a reply, but it was impossible to be sure.

Every instinct screamed at her to rush in and follow that tenuous echo. She cursed silently, knowing to do so would be utterly foolish. Imagining the multitude of possible disasters which might have prevented the boys from making their own way out made the waiting unbearable. Minutes could spell the difference between life and death. Hearing the catch in Tony's voice, she put her arm round his shoulders, comforting herself with the human contact as much as she did him.

Being sensible was the hardest thing.

Being sensible sucked.

A slow eternity passed before help arrived, but in reality the rescuers were remarkably quick. Even before Don radioed the boys were lost in the cave, Constable Madden, using initiative Don later praised him for, had begun combing through the volunteers for those with caving experience.

He appointed John Pedersen, a National Parks ranger who had worked at Jenolan Caves for a time, as the leader. Constable Jasmin Sanjoy and Charlie Reynolds who had both belonged to caving clubs at university, agreed to accompany him underground while Dave Madden himself and an SES crew would support them on the surface.

Kat looked round, hearing heavy boots of the rescue team clattering on the stony floor of the cave.

"Charlie," she breathed, astonished at the relief and trust which surged through her on recognising him, clad in overalls and helmet with an eye-wateringly bright headlamp.

Charlie wouldn't give up till he found her boy. Neither would the others, she realised a moment later.

"We'll bring them back, Kathleen," Charlie murmured, standing beside her as Don made his report and showed John the stringline the boys had left as a guide.

Too emotional for words, Kat nodded and squeezed his hand, forcing a weak smile to her lips.

Moments later she, Tony and Tom were urged outside to wait. It was a beautiful night beside the creek, with the Easter moon rising over the brow of the hill and flowering gums perfuming the soft night air. While men milled around in small groups, talking quietly, Kat sat to one side on a flat rock. Alone. Worrying. *Something* had happened in the depths of the cave, or the boys would have found their own way out. Praying reality wouldn't be as bad as the scenarios conjured up by her too-active imagination, she waited stoically.

Two more vehicles growled their way along the fire trail, claiming the last parking spots left in the small clearing. Lost in her thoughts, Kat didn't look round, so it was with a start of surprise her arms automatically closed around the twins when they threw themselves onto her lap.

"What ...?"

"I brought them, Kat." Maggie Bardon sat heavily beside Kat on her rock, and Ailsa and Mickey huddled at her feet.

"I came back to town as soon as I heard. None of us could bear the waiting at home, so I packed soup and tea into the thermoses and brought the kids to join you. Probably the wrong thing, but I felt at a time like this a family belongs together."

"Right or wrong, I'm glad to see you all, Maggie." Kat hugged her children while Maggie handed round steaming cups of soup.

"The Whitman's came out too, to be with Tony. Everyone else is waiting in town for news, and the Ladies Auxiliary are sending out food for the rescue team."

Time hung heavily as they waited, both families gravitating together in mutual support. In the quiet time after midnight, when the twins had finally fallen asleep wrapped in the rugs Maggie had brought, there was a commotion at the mouth of the cave. Kat sprang to her feet and rushed over, Ailsa and Mickey hard on her heels.

"What is it? Have you found them?" Tony pushed into the space beside her, Marcia holding tightly to his arm.

Jasmine Sanjoy and Don Matthews emerged from the cave together. "Good news, folks," Don said, smiling his relief as he pulled Luke Whitman forward, thrusting him into his parents' arms. "As you can see, they found them, safe and relatively sound. You might like to give this young man the once-over, Doc, just to be sure."

Kat clutched his arm. Duty could wait. Only one boy had been delivered to his waiting family.

"Dennis? What about Dennis, Sergeant?"

"He's coming, Kat. Kids."

Don hitched his belt, putting on his most comforting smile.

"Seems there was a bit of an accident. They were right at the end of their string, ready to turn back, Luke says, when the floor of the cave fell away from under their feet."

Seeing the alarm on their faces, he hastened to reassure them.

"They didn't fall far, but their torches were lost. The rockslide was too unstable for them to climb in the dark. They did the sensible thing, Doc, and waited to be rescued. Jasmine brought Luke out and is taking the stretcher back for Dennis. He's okay, but he hurt his ankle and can't walk. It won't be long now."

"Thanks, Don." Kat's voice was husky with unshed tears of relief. "I'll check Luke over while we wait." She clasped his hand between both of hers, then turned to find Dennis's friend.

Fortunately, nothing was wrong, although he was chilled to the bone. "Take him home and warm him up," she told Marcia. "Watch out for fevers."

"I feel we should wait with you till Dennis is brought out." Marcia's glance towards her car showed how torn she was between getting her chick home and duty to her friend.

"Go," Kat smiled, giving her a little push to get her moving. "We know he's safe, and I've got plenty of people to keep me company."

Marcia, and the rest of the Whitman clan, didn't need to be told twice. Not when Don seconded Kat's urging them to take care of Luke.

Dawn was still a little way off when Dennis was stretchered out of the cave.

"I'm sorry, Kat," he snuffled, wiping his grubby face with an even grubbier sleeve. "We never meant to cause trouble. We were just looking to see if that old bushranger, Captain Thunderbolt had left anything behind to prove he'd been here."

"Like a treasure chest filled with stolen gold and jewels?" scoffed Tom Carey.

Eyes down, Dennis kept quiet.

"I told the two of you he never did any holdups in this area," Tom continued, speaking harshly in his relief, "so there's no way there'd be any loot to find. Silly pair of buggers."

"Okay, Tom," Don Matthews intervened. "They've learnt their lesson, and now we'd better get young Dennis back to town and get that ankle of his seen to."

Before climbing into the police truck, Kat thanked the rescuers, with a special, "I'll be in touch," directed at Charlie Reynolds. Fortunately, the ankle injury was no more than a sprain, and Dennis was out and about within days.

~~~~~

That wasn't quite the last of Dennis and Luke's escapade, however.

As soon as Dennis was on his feet again Don Matthews had both boys, along with Tony, Marcia and Kat, into the police station. Although both boys had been punished with loss of privileges at home, they had begun viewing their exploit with cocky bravado, showing off to their friends. They weren't so cocky when Don finished dressing them down about the waste of the rescuers valuable time and resources, and the danger they'd placed others in by their foolish actions, not to mention the worry for their families.

In tears, they admitted to their crime, swore repentance and promised never to do such a thing again.
~~~~~

"That's all well and good," the sergeant admonished, "but I reckon you need to make reparation. Not money," he shook his head at Tony, who had reached for his wallet, "and it's not your parents' responsibility, either, boys. I'll expect to see you both here at the station every afternoon for the next two weeks. There's plenty needs doing round town, and I'm putting you on my community service program for juvenile offenders."

This was his own specially devised, unofficial program, personally supervised by himself, whereby kids who'd been up to mischief picked up rubbish, weeded civic gardens and generally made themselves useful around town. A program which had full community support.

17

"Hey Charlie."

His Kathleen, as grim and unsmiling as Charlie had ever seen her, walked up to where he was locking the greenhouses after his workers had left for the day. Figuring she'd let him know her decision when she made it, he'd given her time and space to mull over her feelings.

His heart sank.

Hands shoved in the pockets of her jeans, shoulders slumped, she looked as if she'd had to force herself to approach him. As if she knew her answer wouldn't be the one he wanted.

"Kathleen."

Charlie folded her into his arms, kissing her gently.

Kat responded hungrily. Until, a moment later, she turned her head, dragging her lips from his. She let her forehead rest on his shoulder when he kept his arms around her, holding her close. Gradually, her hands came out of her pockets and her arms crept around his waist.

Relieved, Charlie sighed. For a moment there, he'd feared he'd lost her. Now he knew there was still room for hope.

Kat pushed herself upright, locking her eyes onto his.

"I've got things to tell you, Charlie. And questions I'll expect straight answers to. That's if you're still set on marriage?"

She'd thought long and hard about his declaration of love and his offer of marriage. More than anything, she longed to believe him. Believe his love was true. But first, …

"I am. And I agree we need to talk, Love. Come inside. I'll put the kettle on."

Behind his back Kat winced at the endearment but kept her thoughts to herself until they were sitting across the kitchen table from each other, steaming mugs of tea between them.

"You're not taking pity on me because I helped rescue the boys, are you?"

"If I thought you meant that seriously, Reynolds, there'd be no point in us talking. You wouldn't see me for dust." Letting her annoyance show, Kat sipped her tea, not taking her eyes from his till he nodded.

"Yeah, well. I am grateful," she finally conceded. "Course I am, but this is just about us."

She hoped Charlie believed her. She was wasting her time if he didn't.

"While I waited for you to bring those infernal brats out of that cave, I had nothing to do but think. So I thought about you. Us. About what you'd said. About what I want from life." Kat looked up, reassured to see him listening intently.

"I thought about how I trusted you implicitly with my kids, and reckoned maybe I could trust you with myself as well."

"I'm glad to hear that, Kathleen, and you certainly can trust me. With anything. But, before we go any further, there's something *I* need to ask," Charlie interjected.

"Did you mean it literally when you claimed you weren't interested in having babies? Cause if you are, I'm sorry, but I can't give you any. Just want to be upfront with you. I had mumps as a teen and it left me sterile. So. No kids."

"Well, that's one of my questions answered." Kat's lips twisted in a wry smile.

"Not a deterrent, Charlie. I'll come back to that later. I suppose you've had to face a fair bit of rejection because of it? Was that what you meant by saying you were no good to me or any other woman?"

"Yeah. Renee and I ... She was pretty. Sexy. We liked the same things, so we got married in a mad rush. Thought I'd won the bloody jackpot. I was all in. Wanted a houseful of kids. Back then, a family of my own was my big dream. Then, when it was time for the babies, nothing happened. That was when I found out I couldn't. She dumped me, and was pretty nasty about it. Accused me of lying to her. Among other things. She was the first, but she wasn't the last. Seemed all women wanted was babies. After a while it was just easier to forget about marriage and make do with sex when it was on offer."

"Yeah. You were well on the way to becoming a surly old codger." Kat reached across to squeeze his hand, nervously drawing back almost immediately.

"If I did want babies, Charlie, there are other options available, but I reckon my maternal urges have been hijacked by the mob I've taken on."

She sat back, frowning into the mug clasped between her hands.

"So. My story." Kat put the mug down. Looking Charlie in the eye, she fisted her hands on the table, psyching herself up.

"The beginning you know. You've heard the wild stories about me working at the pub. Upstairs as a prostitute, not a dishwasher in the kitchens. Not true, Charlie." She glared at him, daring him to comment. Wisely, he kept his mouth shut. "Some chose to believe it, my father among them." Her lips tightened, pain flashing across her face at the remembered betrayal. She paused, considering how much to tell, then decided to go for broke.

"He came home roaring drunk, shouting accusations. I don't know for sure if he intended to sexually assault me or just give me an almighty thumping. Neither happened, because I beat him to it. I got my hands on Sean's old cricket bat and belted him one over the head. Hit him for six. He went down like a ton of bricks. I thought I'd killed him." She shuddered. "Luckily for me, I hadn't, though he had the mother of all headaches when he came round. I told him what I'd do if he ever laid a hand on me again. He believed me. Life together became an armed standoff. I'd have left then, if I'd had anywhere to go."

She gulped down a mouthful of tea and continued.

"A few days later I was walking home from work, taking the shortcut over the hill. I was ambushed by the Grant twins, the ones who started all the stories and bullied the hell out of me."

Grimacing, she continued.

"No doubt about *their* intentions. I'd taken to carrying a pocket knife, and with that in one hand and a solid stick from a gum tree in the other, I was holding them off as best I could. Afraid they'd lose their licences, Tom Carey and Matt Hendersen had given up driving home from the pub with a belly full of grog. They walked the same route home.as me. Anyway, that night they came across us, saw what was happening, and weighed in on my side."

Seeing Charlie's anger building to an explosion, she patted his hand, calming him.

"It's all right, Charlie. Tom and Matt were younger then. Not at all feeble like now, and together we beat them off. Tom had a word with Fred and Izzy Hayes who had a word with Dad. The upshot was, even though I was still only fourteen, I drove to work and drove Dad, Tom and Matt home. The Grants still made life miserable for me in dozens of ways, but they never tried to attack me physically again."

"So that's why you're so fond of that pair of old reprobates! No-one could figure it out."

"They wouldn't. We all kept our mouths shut. Mr Grant was a dangerous man. It didn't pay to openly cross him. So that's the Oxley Crossing part of my story."

"After that appalling mistreatment it must have been hard to come back, Kathleen. I doubt I could have."

He believes me. He really does.

Kat's tension eased a little. She rewarded him with another of her wry smiles.

"It was hard. I only stayed for the kids, but, you know, Charlie? I've discovered The Crossing is not such a bad place these days. Most of the deadshits have passed on, one way or another. Can I have a refill?" She held out her empty mug. "Then I'll tell you about Bobby."

Charlie slid the full mugs onto the table and reclaimed his chair.

"Bobby was your husband? I heard you'd been married. And divorced. But no-one seems to know more than that."

"And I'd prefer it stay that way, thank you." Kat got her thoughts in order.

"Like you, I thought I'd won the jackpot. Rich, handsome Texan promising me the earth. I'd just finished med school, and his father pulled strings to get me transferred to do my internship and residency in the best hospital in Dallas. Dwayne and Rhoda were tickled pink to have a doctor for a daughter-in-law. Took me a while to figure out Bobby had been sent to Australia to get him out of some sort of trouble. The family owned clubs, and he'd been a naughty boy. Know how to pick them, don't I?"

She took a hasty sip, shaking her head.

"He'd figured a bride he could show off to his parents and their friends would be his entry back into the fold, and it worked like a charm. In no time he was managing a country club outside Dallas, minding his ps and qs and keeping his nose clean like a good boy. But leopards don't change their spots, Charlie. Pity I didn't recognise him as a leopard. I was working insane hours at the hospital, but I was nearly ready to take a break and have the babies we'd deferred till I was fully qualified."

For a moment Kat couldn't go on. She put her head on her clenched fists, holding the grief in.

"Getting sick wasn't in the plan. I had a sexually transmitted disease, Charlie, and I'd only been with the one man since I'd met him. Bobby." She almost spat his name. Almost wept.

"He'd been lonely, he said, blaming me. As if his lousy choices were my fault. I was always at work, he said, so who could blame him for looking elsewhere? Well, I could. And did."

"Damn it all, Kathleen! The man's an idiot!"

Charlie's support brought a grim smile to Kat's lips.

"My sentiments exactly, Charlie. You know, he reckoned it was all just a bit of fun. That it didn't mean anything, because it was *me* he really loved. Bullshit! His excuses didn't wash with me. I was all set to yell and scream and create one hell of a scandal when I got hit with the second barrel."

Charlie's hands itched to teach her bastard of a husband a lesson he'd never forget.

"Penicillin cleared up Bobby's little problem in no time," Kat continued. "I got an infection which laid me up in hospital. The one where I worked, so everyone knew what was wrong with me. I've never been so humiliated in my life."

Bitterness tinged her voice, and she took another time out before she could continue.

Charlie wished even harder he had Bobby in his sights.

He lay a hand on hers, rubbing gently, offering silent comfort. What was there to say that wouldn't sounded like mere lip-service?

This was hardly the time for banal expressions of sympathy.

Appreciative of his discretion, Kat gripped his hand, squeezing tight, then continued.

"A side-effect of the infection was that I couldn't have those babies I'd planned on. Ever. Overnight Dwayne and Rhoda turned their backs on me. Till then they'd been trying to patch things up between us. As if. Not after they learnt there'd be no grandbabies. They couldn't get shot of me fast enough then. Even had a likely replacement lined up ready and waiting. They offered me money to go quietly, Charlie, and to my eternal shame I took it."

Kat grimaced, looking away so Charlie wouldn't see the tears welling in her eyes. She blinked hard, tugged her hand free and took a sip from her cup.

"It cost them though," she added. "They might have bought me off, but I didn't come cheap. A penthouse apartment in a prime location in San Francisco. Fancy car. Strings pulled for a quick transfer to another good hospital, and a fat investment portfolio. I figured I could always use the money to help those in need, and I do, Charlie. Eases my conscience. Anyway, a quickie divorce ended that phase of my far from illustrious history."

"Hell, Kathleen. You've been through more than any one person should have to endure. You're well rid of Bobby and his family."

"Sure am. At least here in The Crossing no-one's hiding behind false smiles. They come right out and say what they think to your face. I'm glad I came home to Australia. But I'm not finished yet, Charlie. There's a bit more left in the dirty secrets department."

"You do know you don't have to bare your soul to me this way, don't you Kathleen. I love you. No ifs, buts or maybes. I love the woman you are today."

"Yeah, I get that Charlie, and you know what? It feels good. Really good. But *I* need you to know the very worst about me."

His acceptance felt so truly heart-warming, Kat almost told him then what she'd realised during those long hours waiting to see him bring Dennis back to her.

No. No yet, she decided. *Not till he knows the whole sordid mess.*

"I'm still going to tell you the lot, though. So you understand exactly what you'll be letting yourself in for with me."

That sounded like the most encouraging thing his Kathleen had said yet. Charlie felt like cheering. Or picking her up and hauling her off to his bedroom to show her unequivocally how he felt about her. But not yet. If she needed to purge the vileness of her past; then the least he could do was listen.

"Tell me the rest, then, Kathleen."

Kat finished her tea, put the mug down carefully, and launched into the final stage of her confession.

"Let's just say, in the aftermath of Bobby's betrayal I made some bad choices. Too many men I shouldn't have looked sideways at. As if I was trying to show him. Huh! I was the only idiot who suffered. And drowning one's sorrows is never such a hot idea. Especially with the Murphy weakness for alcohol. I woke up to myself in time on both counts. Got help. Sorted myself out, and on a wave of homesickness came back to Australia. The rest you know."

Kat stood abruptly, picked up the mugs and took them to the sink.

"Still think I'm a hot prospect in the marriage stakes, Reynolds?" she asked, mocking herself with her derisive tone.

Still, she held her breath, watching Charlie's reflection in the dark glass of the kitchen window, surprised to see night had fallen while she'd spilled her guts.

Figuring actions spoke louder than words, Charlie stood and walked over to Kat. Hands on her shoulders, he turned her to face him, pressing an almost chaste kiss on her lips. He drew back, waited till she raised wary eyes to his, then went down on one knee, holding both her hands in his.

"Kathleen Murphy, you've faced terrible ordeals with great courage and resilience, becoming the strong, honest woman I love with all my heart and soul. Will you do me the great honour of becoming my wife?"

"Get up, you idiot."

Uttered a strangled laugh, Kat hauled him to his feet.

When Charlie would have pulled her into his arms, Kat held him at a distance. Still.

"Now I can tell you, Charlie. Now I know you won't be sticking by me because you feel sorry for me. I …"

"Sorry!" Charlie exclaimed.

"For you, Kathleen? Sure, I'm sorry you've suffered so much during your life, but no way do I feel sorry *for you*! Your strength and resilience make you a woman to be admired and looked up to."

"Oh, Charlie, you're such a good man. Thank you for loving me so selflessly." She wrapped her arms around his neck, putting her heart and soul into her kiss.

"Not yet," she murmured when he made it plain he was ready for more. "Not till I share one more thing with you."

"There's more?" His groan brought a cheeky smile to her lips.

"Not much, Darling, but it's the most important bit. Like I said earlier. While I waited for you out at the cave, I did some thinking. Faced up to my own feelings. Decided what I truly want. My life has been turned upside down since I came home, and my emotional needs and aspirations along with it. I've changed. I realised something I've been too scared to admit, even to myself."

Kat locked eyes with her lover. She didn't want him to miss a syllable of what she was about to say.

"If you're absolutely, one hundred percent sure you want to marry me, then that's what I'd like too, because you see, Charlie Reynolds, I love you. Love you! Love you! Love you!"

If anyone had been passing by, Charlie's joyous whoop would have made them smile. He picked Kat up in his arms, whirling her round and round.

"Kathleen, my love, those are the most beautiful words I've ever heard, and, yes! I am absolutely, one hundred percent sure I want to marry you, Kathleen. More sure than I've ever been of anything in my life."

"Then, yes. I'll be proud and happy to marry you, Charlie Reynolds. Just as soon as I can. Because I love you."

Kat couldn't say those words often enough, having feared she'd never say them to a man again.

Kat carried high in Charlie's arms, their lips locked, they were on the way to the bedroom when Kat's phone rang.

Bumping foreheads, they both cursed, then Kat wriggled free and ran back to answer it.

"Gotta go, Charlie. Downside of being a country doctor. Sorry. Brenda Foster's son has taken a bad spill off his quad bike."

It wasn't till the next evening Kat and Charlie had their belated, and very private, celebration.

18

"Listen up, everyone. I've got a Very Important Announcement to make."

"What sorta announcement, Kat?"

"Dennis!" Kat mock-sighed. "Kids, please tell your brother what I just said."

Four voices chanted in unison. "Listen up!"

"Especially you, Den," Ailsa added, just to be sure he got the point.

"Thanks," Kat laughed. "So. My announcement. You may have noticed I've invited Charlie to dinner tonight. There's a particular reason for that."

"We just thought it was because he's our friend."

"He is our friend, Estelle, but soon he's going to be even more."

Maggie, seated at the end of the table opposite Kat, guessed what was coming and clapped her hands.

It was only with difficulty she held back her comments, so as not to spoil Kat's surprise.

With a quick wink at Maggie, Kat reached a hand down to Charlie, drawing him up to stand at her side.

"Kids, Charlie and I love each other, and we've decided to get married."

Kat's last words were drowned out in cheers and happy exclamations. The next few minutes were a noisy jumble of hugs, kisses and congratulations.

"Kat! Kat!" Dennis tugged on his sister's arm, pulling her down so he could whisper in her ear. A whisper clearly audible to the others crowding round them.

"Kat, Charlie's only going to be our brother, isn't he? After you get married. He's not going to be our father, is he?"

"Idiot!" Mickey hugged his brother reassuringly, before Kat could answer. "Of course he won't be our father."

"Mickey's right, Dennis." This time it was Charlie himself pre-empting Kat. "Technically, I'll be your brother-in-law. I'll be helping Kathleen take good care of you all, but I won't treat you harshly as your father did. That's not my style. Like Kathleen, I believe in raising children with love and understanding."

"Even if we're naughty?"

"Especially if you're naughty, Den."

Kat finally got a word in.

"You remember what I told you? If you deserve punishment, we'll negotiate a suitable punishment together. That still goes."

Dennis nodded slowly. By either luck or being on his best behaviour, the only punishment he'd incurred had been for not asking permission or telling where he was going the day he and Luke got lost in the cave. And his punishment, being grounded, with no computer game time, had been the result of a discussion between himself and his sister. That particular punishment had been his suggestion, and she'd agreed. She'd even shortened the time he'd volunteered since it was his first offence.

"The same rules as now will still apply after Charlie comes to live here. The biggest difference will be, you'll have two adults to answer to instead of one, but you'll also have two adults to love you and care for you and stand up for you."

"Then I guess it'll be okay if you marry him, Kat."

"Thanks Mate." Charlie ruffled Dennis's hair, bringing a smile to a face too solemn for such a happy occasion.

It wasn't till she was tucking them in bed that the twins asked a question they'd been discussing privately after dinner.

"Kat. After the wedding, you'll be Kathleen Reynolds."

Kat nodded. She hadn't considered the name change herself, but it was true, and she wouldn't mind being shot of the name 'Murphy' one little bit. Dr Reynolds had a nice ring to it, now she thought about it.

"And," Clarice took over from her sister, "we wondered if it means we get to change our names, too."

"Yeah," Estelle cut in. "Our friend Gwynna changed her name when her mother got married. She used to be Gwyneth Smith and now she's Gwyneth Lambert. So, are we going to be Clarice and Estelle Reynolds after you and Charlie get married?"

Another possibility I haven't considered. And why shouldn't they want a new name to go with their new start with me? Us.

"Would you like that, Estelle? Clarice?"

Kat looked from one little girl to the other. Both nodded vigorously.

"Okay, girls. No promises, mind. I'll have to discuss this with Charlie first, but I'll see what he says."

She kissed them both goodnight and went to talk to the other children, who, being older, were allowed to stay up later.

"So what do you think?" she asked, after explaining the twins' suggestion.

"Great idea!" Mickey was all for it. "It will make Charlie feel more like our brother, won't it?

"I agree. I'd like to be Ailsa Reynolds. Some of the kids who aren't my friends sneer when they say 'Murphy'. They won't sneer at 'Reynolds'."

"It'll make us a proper family. All of us with the same name."

"You're right, Dennis. Well, that settles it. I'll talk to Charlie. Good thing he hasn't left yet."

Charlie, who'd discreetly gone for a wander in the garden when Kat said she wanted a private word with the children, was feeling more nervous by the minute. The kids had seemed to accept him, quite enthusiastically, in fact, but if there was a problem, ...

"I know it's a bit chilly outside but come and sit in the summer house for a bit, Charlie. The kids have a request they'd like me to run by you."

Charlie relaxed. A request sounded a whole lot better than a problem.

"So, what do they want? The cathedral with the archbishop presiding?"

"Nothing so flash." Kat shuddered. A big wedding was so not to her taste. "Actually, it sounds simple, but it's really important for quite a few reasons. They want to know if they can change their names. If we can all be called 'Reynolds'?"

"I don't see why not? They can do it unofficially right away, till we make it legal. I'll check out the process if you like."

"That'd be good, Darling." Kat rewarded him suitably for his easy co-operation.

"You know, Charlie?" she said a while later. "All this talk about changing names made me think of something you said a while back. About a family of your own being one of your dreams," she added when he raised a questioning brow. "The kids are my family. Of my blood, if not of my body. I'll be sharing them with you, you realise? They'll be your family, too."

"Sure. I'm looking forward to being part of your family, Kathleen. It'll be like having children of my own. I already love them, you know."

The subject was dropped then as they were both intent on communicating in ways other than verbal.

The following night Charlie was once again a dinner guest, and this time he was the one to ask for a family meeting after the meal was cleared away.

"Kids. Kathleen. About this name change idea."

A couple of nervous frowns met his opening words, so he was quick to reassure them all.

"I'm all for it. I think being the Reynolds family, all together, is a wonderful idea. Only, I've been thinking it over today. We can do better than simply changing your names. If you like, Kathleen and I can adopt you all. We'd be your parents, Dennis, but you can trust us to be good parents. Not a mother and father, I know you don't want that, but more than a brother and sister. Parents. The adults responsible for your welfare. What do you think?"

"Adopt them?"

"Yes." Charlie looked nervously at Kat. "I know I should have talked it through with you first, instead of just blurting out my grand idea, Kathleen darling."

"Umm. You should have. In this case I'll let you off," she smiled her quirky lop-sided grin. "Actually, the idea has merit. It would cement us more closely together as a family, wouldn't it? What do you kids think? You're all old enough to decide such an important issue for yourselves, you know, and Charlie and I will go along with the majority decision."

Charlie was inclined to argue his case, but reluctantly nodded. Shared decision-making was one of the family practices he'd agreed to.

"Can we talk it over together, Kat?"

"Of course, Mickey. You can have all the time you need. Any questions, don't be afraid to ask."

The younger children trailed after Mickey to the upstairs sitting area which Kat had given them for their own.

"Think they'll take long to decide?"

What Charlie really wanted to ask was, did Kathleen think the children would agree to being adopted, but he was wary of tempting fate.

"Not if they're as much like me as I think they are, Darling. They know their own minds. Just give them a bit of space to talk it over and reach their own conclusions."

She leaned over to kiss him, then sat back and picked up her cup of tea. She was putting the empty tea cups in the dishwasher a little later when she heard the clatter of feet on the stairs.

"We're back Kat," Ailsa called.

"I'll be right with you."

When Kat returned to the lounge room, the children were circled around the sofa, Mickey on an ottoman pulled up in front of Charlie, and the others on the floor to either side of him. She slipped into the space left for her beside Charlie.

"Okay," Mickey began nervously. "We've talked over this adoption idea and come to a decision."

He looked at his younger siblings in turn, receiving an affirmative nod from each. He held his right arm out in front of him, clenched fist facing down. Four smaller hands reached out, slapping down on top of his. Five pairs of eyes locked on Kat and Charlie.

"One for all, ..." they intoned in unison.

Kat had seen them do this before but had never been invited to participate. Now, if their stares meant what she thought they did, she and Charlie were being included in the ritual.

She added her hand to the stack.

Charlie, catching on quickly, joined with them, and the two of them completed the oath in ringing tones.

"… and all for one!"

"We agree to the adoption," Ailsa added, "in case you hadn't realised."

The next minute they were locked in a group hug.

"Kat, you're crying! Aren't you happy?"

"So happy there's no words to express how I feel, Clarice. I arrived home in The Crossing with an empty heart. Now, between the five of you and Charlie, it's filled to overflowing with love I thought was beyond my reach." She sobbed, reaching for a clean handkerchief to dry her eyes.

"So why are you crying?"

"Oh, Dennis. These are rainbow tears. There are no rainbows without rain and sometimes deep happiness is the same. See. If you look, I'm smiling through the tears like a rainbow in a sun shower."

~~~~~

Since neither Kat nor Charlie saw any reason to wait longer than the minimum one month before they married, and neither wanted all the frills and excesses of a traditional wedding, the restrictions placed on gatherings gave them an irrefutable excuse to forego the fuss. A wedding pared down to the barest essentials was easy to organise in the short time.
~~~~~

It was a true family celebration, held at home.

A visit to *Kit & Kaboodle* in Peel Street produced new outfits all round, and Maggie cooked up a storm. Even if the wedding was to be held at home with only family in attendance, she was determined no-one would be able to cast aspersions on the catering.

Wanting to be part of the celebrations, their friends insisted on making their own contributions. Geoff Tan baked his super-special fruit cake, and Jean Bowen who'd been the reigning show champion for the last six years, decorated it. Thea Marten thrilled the twins with the hair styles she devised to compliment their new dresses, and Eddie Patterson worked her usual magic with the flowers. All very much as it would have been for a larger event.

The groom was judged film-star handsome in his Armani suit, and there were oohs and aahs of appreciation when the bride, Paris chic in a white linen and lace suit bought online, was led out by her three young sisters, the boys having elected to support the groom.

"Bit like a modern Brady Bunch, ain't they?" Matt Henderson whispered to his mate, Tom Carey.

"And every bit as happy, I reckon," Tom whispered back, "which is just as it should be."

Reverend Charles, the Anglican minister, had consented to officiate even though the ceremony was held on Kat's front veranda so those friends who couldn't be invited but wanted to be there anyway could 'exercise' on the street and watch from an approved distance.

Sergeant Don Matthews, interpreting the law with a liberal hand since The Crossing had registered no cases of the virus, just happened to wander by to ensure social distancing was adhered to.

When Eddie Patterson, dressed as finely as she would have been at any other, more conventional, wedding, heard a comment about it being a dismal affair, she had her answer ready.

"Dismal? Not a bit of it. Just look at those beaming smiles. This is one of the happiest weddings I've seen. Besides, this is Oxley Crossing. We can be counted on to do things differently here."

"Sure can. Wouldn't miss this wedding for quids," Bill Whitman stated, backing her up.

All in all, those whose opinions mattered were unanimous.

If the bride and groom were as much in love as Kat and Charlie, pomp and ceremony simply didn't matter. It was the marriage, not the wedding, which was most important.

The bride and groom, hand in hand, were about to head out to the Morgan's holiday retreat just downsteam from Rainbow Falls for the brief honeymoon which was all they had time for, when the phone rang. Kat groaned, answering anyway. It would be just her luck to be called out on an emergency.

It *was* just her luck, but instead of the expected emergency, it was the gift to top all gifts.

"Dr Murphy, I am Dr Ravi Gandhi. I wonder if the position you advertised for an assistant doctor in your Oxley Crossing medical practice is still open ...?"

~~~~~

In a few short weeks Dr Gandhi was explaining to the curious why he and his wife Sandra, whom he introduced as his surfer chick child bride, to most people's amusement, had decided to relocate their family.

"We were not comfortable living in Melbourne with all these lockdowns." He said. "It did not feel at all safe for us or our children, you know. After careful consideration we chose to move to the countryside. Oxley Crossing seems a pleasant town in which to raise a family. The climate is better than Melbourne's, too."

Oxley Crossing agreed that it was, indeed, a good place for families, and Dr and Mrs Gandhi and their three children were made thoroughly welcome.

"Takes the pressure off our Dr Kat," Bill Whitman summed up. "Might as well give the chap a fair trial."
~~~~~

Epilogue

On the first anniversary of Kat and Charlie's wedding, the auditorium at the Oxley Crossing Bowling Club was filled to bursting with guests who hadn't been able to attend the wedding. With the borders open, Charlie's parents in Queensland and his brother in South Australia had made the journey to Oxley Crossing to celebrate with him and meet Kat and the children for the first time.

Bridget, Pat, Sean and all their families were together again for the first time too, since the funeral, and celebrated with contented hearts, glad to see how well life had worked out for Kat and the children from such shaky beginnings.

"Okay," Charlie, walking onto the stage with Kathleen, tapped the microphone for attention. When the noise level abated enough for him to make himself heard, he thanked all their guests for coming and for their friendship and support throughout the previous year.

"… Now I've got an extra special announcement. Come on up here, kids," he called, waving them forward.

"As you all know, we're not quite the average family."

Amid the laughter and comments his statement generated, he and Kathleen joined hands with the children as they arrived at their sides.

"Here we are, folks. Our whole family. And just to make it official, Kathleen and I have adopted these children. The paperwork has finally been delivered, and I reckon that's another wonderful reason to celebrate. I give you a toast; The Reynolds Family."

While everyone else drank to them, they raised their joined hands high and shouted their family motto.

"All for one, and one for all"

Thank you for reading

Healing Dr Murphy.

I do hope you enjoyed it. Perhaps you would like to leave a review on Amazon, Goodreads or your favourite review site to help other readers find my books. It needn't be more than a few words, but it makes such a difference for me and reviews are a great way for readers to connect with writers.

I love receiving feedback from readers and answer all emails at

lenawestauthor@gmail.com

I have lots more stories to come, even another few in the Oxley Crossing series. That town keeps drawing me back for just one more story.

So, sign up for my newsletter at

www.lenawestauthor.com

to be first to hear about my new releases.

Here is Your Preview of
The Wyldeflower Series Book 1

BURIED TRUTH

1

Christmas Day

"So, Mum, when can we break out the bubbly? We've opened all the presents, and thanks again for the lovely loot. We've cleared away the wrappings. What are we waiting for?"

Forest, at twenty-one the youngest of the six Wylde siblings —named, in alphabetical order from eldest to youngest, for Australian wildflowers - was always the most impatient.

He couldn't wait to move on to the next item on their traditional Family Christmas agenda; namely, the serious eating and drinking. And maybe trouncing his sisters at boules by way of a diversion.

"Oh, just one more little thing first," Daisy Wylde smiled mysteriously and assembled the family for her big announcement.

"Eremaea. Acacia. Correa. Out of the kitchen and join us all here in the lounge. The turkey can wait a bit longer to go in the oven. I … Your father and I, that is, …"

"Leave me out, Love. This is all your doing,"

Laughing, Eucalypt Wylde – Cal – was quick to dissociate himself.

"Yes. Well," Daisy continued without missing a beat. "As I was saying, I have an extra, very special, gift for each of you, my darlings. I'm giving you each a licence to dream."

"Isn't that what you call your Lotto entries?" Eremea chipped in. "Your licence to dream?"

"Do you want us to take over buying the family tickets?" asked Correa. "I thought you got a kick out of buying them yourself."

"Is something wrong? Why can't you buy them yourself as always, Mum?"

Alarmed, Dianella, who hadn't really been paying attention, being too busy paging through the Nigella Lawson cookbook her brother had given her, immediately feared a worst-case scenario.

Impatiently, Daisy huffed, clapping her hands. "If you would all stop interrupting, I might get a word in edgeways and *tell you*."

"All ears, Mum."

"Yes Forest, darling, I see them flapping. Be careful not to get caught in a high-wind area. All of you," she snapped, including even her grinning husband in her glaring roundup, "have always scoffed at me for wasting my money on Lotto, but, ..."

And here the whole family joined in reciting the familiar refrain.

"... the fortune teller foretold a big win, as long as I was patient and believed in it."

Silence – rare when the Wyldes were gathered together – reigned for a long, pregnant moment.

"Bloody hell, Mum!" Forest, first to connect the dots, exclaimed. "Do you mean to say you've finally won something!"

"More than the usual pitiful five or ten dollars?"

Eremaea stared at her mother, mouth open till she remembered and snapped it shut.

Cal was doubled over holding his stomach, he was laughing so hard. He loved his wife and children dearly, and always found them the best entertainment to be had in the state of Victoria, if not the whole of Australia. True individuals, every single one of them. How could they not be, with the unusual names he'd bestowed on them, tributes to his and his Daisy's unconventional upbringing in a Nimbin commune?

This Christmas Day was proving to be exceptionally entertaining, and it had only just begun.

Daisy rolled her eyes.

"Oh ye of little faith," she intoned portentously, her mouth twitching at the corners.

"Yes! Yes I did!"

She gave up trying to be solemn and laughed aloud.

"My numbers finally came in. I was sole winner of the big one last month. Thirty million plus."

Eyes dancing, she sat back, hands folded demurely in her lap, anticipating an uproar. She was not disappointed.

"Thirty Million? Dollars?"

"Yes, Acacia. Australian dollars, that is."

"Plus, Acacia," Dianella corrected her sister. "Don't forget the plus. Plus by how much, Mum?"

"Last month?" The dollars were too mind-blowing for Correa. "You've been sitting on this stupendous news for a month? And you didn't *tell* us? Didn't you think we'd be *interested*?"

"What do you plan to do with so much money?"

"Well, Eremaea dear, that's what we want to talk to all of you about, if you'd all just *listen*."

"Listening." Forest drew his fingers across his lips in a zipping motion and sat up like an obedient five-year-old.

Astounded, his five older sisters slowly followed suit.

Cal swallowed his laughter and nodded to his wife to go ahead.

"Okay. Well, it's more money than your father and I could ever spend, although we've got exciting plans for some of it. We're sharing what's left with the six of you. It's not for you to go off on a wild spending spree and end up worse off in six months. It's so you can pursue your dreams and not get stuck in jobs you hate just so you can pay the rent. We want you to live happy, fulfilled lives."

She gazed at the stunned faces of her beloved Wyldeflower Bouquet as she'd long ago dubbed her children with their pretty wildflower names. Even Forest, who was named for the Forest Red Gum, her favourite tree, beneath which where he'd been conceived one memorable holiday. Which led to his sisters nicknaming him Gumby.

"Dream big, darlings," Daisy, teary-eyed, commanded.

"Don't settle for second best."

February

"Ooh, Boronia, I'm so mad I could spit. That promotion should have been mine. I had it in the bag, and more than that, I worked hard for it. I deserved it."

Acacia Wylde ran both hands through her winter-grass brown hair, pushing it up into unruly spikes.

"That's the promotion to Team Leader?" Boronia, long, runner's legs swung over the arm of the sofa, tore her attention away from *Hidden Valley* to see what her sister was so riled up about.

"Yes. The promotion that ought by rights to be mine," Acacia hissed through gritted teeth.

"You really thought your misogynistic dinosaur of a boss would promote you, or any woman, over the head of his very own arse-licking nephew?" Boronia snorted, blowing blonde wisps out of her eyes. "Get real, girl. You may have deserved it, but you had less than an ice-cream's chance in Hell of getting it."

Acacia slung her briefcase into the corner and herself into her favourite armchair, the belligerence leaking out of her faster than the stuffing from her favourite old teddy bear when her sister's red Kelpie pup, Merlot, had mauled it last week.

"Yeah. You're right."

Acknowledging defeat, Acacia slumped in her chair, burying her face in a cushion until she recalled an even bigger insult.

"You know what else, Bron? Old Misery Guts had the hide to offer me the position of personal assistant to his damned nephew. Which translates to me doing the work and him stealing the credit. Even Mr Hayden knows dear James," she drew the name out derisively, "will never cope on his own. I have till Friday to accept; or be moved sideways into Human Resources. Which would effectively be a demotion with lower pay."

Sympathetic as she was, Boronia still couldn't hold back a spurt of hastily swallowed laughter at the idea of her hot-headed older sister working in a position requiring tact and diplomacy. She was brilliant in Advertising, but Human Resources ...?

"Sounds to me as if he'd really like to give you the shove if you won't kowtow."

Acacia stewed in silence while Boronia, recognising a crisis requiring more than verbal sympathy, poured red wine into their best glasses. One of the *good* bottles from *Wolf Blass.* This was too serious an occasion for *Chateau Casque.*

"I've got a good mind to tell them to stick their job," Acacia muttered, her face once again buried in the cushion she held in her arms to soak up the silent tears dribbling down her cheeks.

"Why don't you?" Boronia handed her a glass. "You've got that money from Mum's Lotto win. Tell them to shove the job. Mum said the money is to make our dreams come true. That we should dream big."

She hesitated, then broached the subject her sister had declared off-limits.

"Take some time out and write your bloody book, Acacia, instead of dreaming about doing it 'one day'. Stop making excuses, Cacia. Thanks to Mum, you can afford the time to find out if you've got it in you to succeed as a writer."

Acacia spluttered on a mouthful of shiraz. She'd been dreaming of being a writer since primary school, only there was always study, or work, or something which was maybe fear, getting in the way. Boronia was the only one in the family who knew her dream, and that was because they had once shared a room and now shared a house, and her sister snooped.

"I've read some of what you've written Cacia," Boronia said, confirming her sister's frequent accusations. She snooped. Shamelessly. She'd never denied it.

How else could she learn her sisters' deepest, darkest secrets? And Boronia, although the kindest and most reliable of sisters, had a voracious curiosity.

"You're good," she added in her most encouraging tone. "Really good, Cacia. *I* believe you can do it, and now's the perfect time to give it your best shot, don't you reckon?"

"Do you really believe I can?"

If there was one thing Acacia could count on in life, it was her sisters telling the truth. All of them were blunt and to the point. If Bron said she could do it, then maybe …?

"Only one way to find out, isn't there?"

"Damn right! I'll do it Bron. I'll hand in my resignation tomorrow and I'll write my book!"

Suddenly her anger and depression fled as if they'd never existed. Acacia's warm, cinnamon eyes sparkled with excitement and enthusiasm.

Boronia leant over to clink her glass against her sister's.

"Here's to the next runaway success story. Surely that's a big enough dream to satisfy even Mum."

***

March

"Bron, can I run something by you?"

Boronia slipped a bookmark between the pages and sat up, looking enquiringly towards her sister.

"Fire away, Acacia."

"Well, as you know, I'm making the wreck of the *Ly-ee-Moon* a central feature of my book." Boronia nodded, so Acacia continued. "I've been doing some research, and I discovered something interesting. While not all passengers and crew were accounted for among those recovered from the wreck, either alive or dead, it seems there may, possibly, have been others no-one knew about at all."

"How could that happen? Were there stowaways?"

"No. Not stowaways. Apparently, latecomers could jump on board at the last minute. They didn't have cabins and weren't always added to the passenger manifest."

"Sounds shonky to me."

"Me too, but I figured it left a nice gap to slip my fictional characters into the true shipwreck story. Then today, I was doing a very wide search, and I came across one of these stray passengers. An actual one. Julian Morton. His wife claimed he left Melbourne on the *Ly-ee-Moon* and was never heard from again. No body recovered from the wreck. She went to court to have him declared dead so she could take over the family business. Since there were witnesses, the judge upheld her claim."

"Interesting. But what's your problem? As I see it, this story will make yours appear more authentic."

"Yes. ... Yes, it will, but Bron, I can't help wondering if there might be an even more interesting story I can use. Do you think it'd be okay if I did a bit of investigating? You know, the who, how, when, what etc?"

"Why ever not? He's been dead over a hundred years."

Fondling Merlot's soft, red ears, Boronia looked enquiringly at her sister.

"I'm just worried there might be descendants who would be offended."

"Easy. Shove in a disclaimer and change the names to protect the innocent. I see that in lots of the books I read. What do you want him for, anyway?"

"That's why they might be offended. I'm going to murder him," Acacia stated cheerfully. "He's the perfect murder victim, don't you think? Then, trying to escape, his killer can go down with the ship. This story is going to have it all, Bron. Murder, romance, betrayal and skulduggery. Maybe even a happy ending," she laughed.

Boronia laughed with her. She thought her sister was spot on.

"Just be careful not to confuse the readers by having too much going on. Remember the KISS principle, Cacia." Settling back into her chair, she opened her book, leaving Acacia to her exciting mystery man.

Continued.......

To get

Buried Truth

as soon as it's released – go to

www.lenawestauthor.com

and make sure that you are signed up for news and release notices!

Other Books by
Lena West

Historical Romances

Unto Death

In Colonial society of the 1860s marriage is a contract unto death; and scandal is death of another kind.

Can Lucy and Stephen find happiness together in spite of the odds stacked against them?

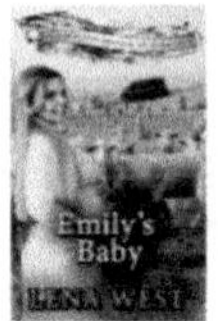 **Emily's baby**

https://www.amazon.com/dp/B07TPDN13W

In the 1950s an unwed mother needed help if she was to keep her child. Emily had no family, and no money, but she would do whatever it took to keep her precious baby.

 **Home is the Heart**

https://www.amazon.com/dp/B08G179HMX

Eliza risks all, travelling, with the husband she loves, half way round the world in search of the home and family of her own for which her heart yearns. They arrive just in time to be swept up in the gold rush, only to meet with tragedy.

Alone, with more than herself to consider, Eliza accepts a marriage of convenience with a New Norcia farmer. With a vengeful woman intent on tearing their fragile little family apart, only time will tell if Eliza can find happiness at *Wattle Bend* with her new family

Contemporary Romances

Loving Fenella

https://www.amazon.com/dp/B07B3RLS98/

When artist and teacher, Fenella Wilkins, is inspired to paint Greg Kendall, she falls in love with both him and his daughter, Aimee. But he is engaged to the beautiful model, Linda Beck. It is against Fen's principles to poach another woman's man, even when self-centred Linda is the other woman.

Forgotten

https://www.amazon.com/dp/B083Y2ZR28

When a soldier returns from the front minus his memory, is he the same man he was when he left? How can Krista be sure which man she really loves?

Contemporary Series

Love in Oxley Crossing Series

In the rural town of Oxley Crossing, love is in the air, and romance triumphs, no matter the challenges.

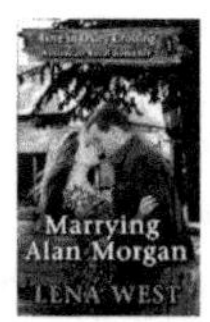 **Marrying Alan Morgan**

https://www.amazon.com/dp/B0774V1L25/

Sparks fly when a feisty red-haired city girl with a past that makes it hard to trust, meets a bitter, disillusioned farmer who's sure love isn't worth the effort. But sometimes, the heart knows better than the mind.

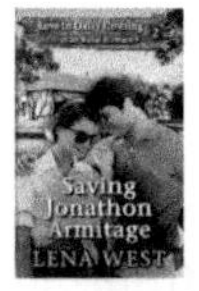 **Saving Jonathon Armitage**

https://www.amazon.com/dp/B0788GCQJQ

A woman home again for family, a man sworn to moving on. Jealousy, distrust and misdirection, must all be overcome before two lives can be transformed by love.

Finding Mr Wright

https://www.amazon.com/dp/B07C98B7PJ

Escaping her violent ex-husband by claiming sanctuary in Oxley Crossing is the best decision Geni Sullivan has ever made – for herself and her son, nine-year-old Jamie.

Electing Robert Whitman

https://www.amazon.com/dp/B07KWKLJG6

At the second wedding in a matter of months, Sophie James is seated next to the man she had a teenage crush on. A single, unattached man to whom she is still very attracted. When she returns to The Crossing to help her mother, she decides to take a chance on him.

Redeeming Josh Marten

https://www.amazon.com/dp/B07RNHBYG7

Opposites attract when vibrant, outgoing Thea Benson meets withdrawn, curmudgeonly sculptor, Josh Marten, but behind her bubbly image, Thea is not who she appears to be.

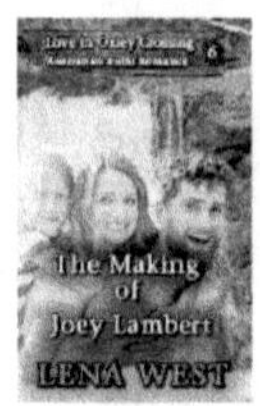

The Making of Joey Lambert

https://www.amazon.com/dp/B088D6RHKD

It is said strong women are not simply born; they are made that way by the storms they walk through. Sienna Smith has survived a category five personal cyclone, but at tremendous cost. One step at a time she's clawed her way back, however, she believes that last difficult step, the one back to 'normal', is beyond her. Not even love for kind, gentle Joey Lambert can carry her that far.

The Wyldeflower Series

Buried Truth (Coming soon)

About the Author

Born in tropical North Queensland, Lena loves living close to the sea, although she moved frequently during her early years, living everywhere from large cities to isolated farms. Her most recent home has a deck overlooking the water, which is her favourite room in the house, for reading, writing, art, craft or even birdwatching, when the local birds come to visit.

After working as a teacher in both Queensland and New South Wales, she took a very early retirement to travel Australia in a motorhome. This idyllic lifestyle lasted several years, during which time she began creating stories and characters, culminating in the fulfillment of her lifelong ambition to write.

Storytelling came naturally - she had been making up stories for her own entertainment all her life, but it wasn't until she began traveling that Lena had time to write down some of her favourites. She writes contemporary romances, including the popular *Love in Oxley Crossing* series, and Australian historical romances.

With an addiction to happily-ever-afters, in both her reading and her own stories, the romance genre was a natural fit, and the variety of places she has lived have all contributed to the settings in which she brings love to life.

You can find Lena on Facebook at:

https://www.facebook.com/LenaWestAuthor

or sign up for her newsletter at:

www.lenawestauthor.com